Iron Will

Book 2 of The Pandora Chronicles

Rebecca Flynn

Black Rose Writing | Texas

ISBN: 978-1-68433-655-5
PUBLISHED BY BLACK ROSE WRITING
www.blackrosewriting.com

Printed in the United States of America
Suggested Retail Price (SRP) $17.95

Iron Will is printed in Calluna

*As a planet-friendly publisher, Black Rose Writing does its best to eliminate unnecessary waste to reduce paper usage and energy costs, while never compromising the reading experience. As a result, the final word count vs. page count may not meet common expectations.

To my parents...

From the time that I was little, you told me that I could do what I wanted with my life and you would always stand proudly beside me. No matter what decisions I've made, you have kept true to those words. You raised me to be strong and to work hard, but also to never be too proud to ask for a helping hand. I have made it this far not because you pushed me, but because you walked beside me, cheering me on the whole time. Thank you.

Iron Will

Prologue

Soft candlelight twinkled as it barely filled the center of the room. Plush leather chairs sat around a large wooden table. The curtains had been drawn and all exits securely locked.

"I feel that we need to discuss the overall usefulness of these so-called 'hunters' that we currently have in our employ," one man said. His face was partially in shadow, but his Spanish accent was very distinct.

The other man nodded in agreement from the shadows. "Some of them follow orders and stick to what we ask, but others." He paused. "It seems like more work to watch them and keep them in line," he added in a clearly British tongue. "These younger Council members come in and try to take over with these ridiculous ideas on how we should run things. The Council has functioned for centuries before them and we will continue." He paused again. "When our way has worked for so long, why should we change it?" He leaned forward into the light. The Venerated One placed his palms together with his index fingers against his lips. He sat lost in thought for a moment. The room was silent. Then, with a sigh, he said, "We cannot just stop contacting them. They will become suspicious and we absolutely cannot have them revealing our existence. We operate in the shadows. The public must not know what we do. It would be detrimental to the church."

"Perhaps we take them out of the picture completely, one by one. Nobody can win every fight. Even hunters can lose from time to time," the other man said. "My Garduna can take care of it for you, as they have in the past for The Council. Your hands will remain clean and none will know."

The Venerated One nodded. "I appreciate your enthusiasm. La Garduna has been loyal over the centuries and never let us down. But we must look at this differently. If we begin to target each of them directly, we will become the targets. No, we must be more creative, secretive, in our approach."

Silence took a seat at the table and watched as the two men pondered their dilemma. It felt as if everything had stopped. Not a heartbeat could be heard, not a breath. Neither man was new to this line of work. The head of La Garduna had not changed in at least a decade and the Venerated One had worked his way up to his title over many years. He had served the previous Venerated One faithfully and creatively. When the time came for a new head of the Council, he was an easy choice.

Now, he reached deep into his mind to handle what he considered just another bump in the road. Several thoughts crossed his mind, but they all resulted in the same thing.

"One day in the future we will need to take these hunters out of the picture. While we could assassinate them individually, the others will hear of it. There must be another way," the Venerated One said to himself. He lifted his head and slow smile spread across his lips. "I believe I have a way to handle this without the others knowing who targeted them. Not only will they not know but if needed, we could keep it a secret from the other Council members as well." He paused again. "If needed."

"What is it? What can we do?" the other man asked eagerly.

"We have already started," he answered. "We've collected creatures to research them and explore the possibilities of their uses in our other ventures. Therefore," he leaned back in his chair. "We select the creatures that can be used to hunt our hunters. We train them and prepare them to take care of our little problem." He smiled. "They become weapons for us."

"By the time they put everything together, the creature has confronted them and eliminated our dependence on them. If the others catch wind of the incident, it will just look like an accident during a job. Excellent," the other man answered.

"We can take this to certain members of the Council, but we must be careful. Not everyone will be behind us," the Venerated One said. "We must go to the ones we are sure of first. We will leave the younger ones out of this venture. They would not understand."

The two men shook hands in the candlelight. With their discussion completed, they snuffed out the candles and quietly left the room one at a time.

Chapter 1

The early December sun sparkled off piles of snow giving them an almost metallic sheen. Icicles twinkled as golden rays passed through them. The air was crisp and silent.

In an explosion of dead leaves and bark, a dog burst from the trunk of a nearby tree. Its tongue hung from the side of its mouth as it raced over the newly fallen powder. Haydeez kicked up puffs of snow as she followed, her eyes trained on the dog. Snow covered her moccasins and the cuff of her jeans. Her long coat flapped behind her as she ran. They weaved back and forth around tree trunks and dead branches. The canine gave a quick bark that sounded almost like a laugh and ran head first into a large oak tree.

Haydeez skidded to a halt and touched the tree. She cried out in frustration. "Seriously! Would you stop that already?" She spun around to look for the creature. Heat rose from her body as she growled under her breath.

A twig snapped and leaves exploded about twenty yards away. The dog burst from another tree and yipped with glee.

"Bad dog! I've had enough of your little games." She pulled a large shotgun from a holster on her back and took off at a sprint. She cocked the gun and aimed. "This had better work," she mumbled and fired.

The gun boomed. The echo caused snow to sprinkle down all around her. A single bullet exploded from the barrel. As it flew through the air, pieces of the casing fell away to expose the heart of the projectile: a dull grey dust. When the dust came in contact with the dog, it yelped and tripped over a branch. It tumbled into a tree trunk with a thump and whimpered.

She ran up to the creature and chuckled. "No more tree hopping for you today, Fido. Time to go to your new home." She reached into an inner pocket in her jacket and pulled out a small item. With a flick of her wrists, a net draped over the canine and she wrapped it up with minimal effort. Its green and brown fur poked out of the holes. She hoisted the creature onto her shoulder and made her way through the trees.

"Lead dust works on Hoko," she said. "I guess they're magical enough to be susceptible to the lead and stop that annoying but nifty little tree walk thing they do. I'm almost to the Jeep. I have to make a quick stop to drop off the pooch, but I'll probably be home late tonight."

A voice answered in her earpiece. "How late is late? Should I keep the fire going and wait on dinner or will this be another of those 'fend for yourself' evenings?" Linx asked.

She laughed. "You do know you don't have to wait for me to eat right? Do you starve yourself every time I make a trip without you?" She pulled her keys out of her pocket and unlocked the Jeep. The creature whimpered again. "Hush, you've caused enough trouble today." She placed it onto the back seat and closed it up. "Ugh, I hate when they look at me with those pleading eyes. Stop making me feel guilty," she yelled through the back window. "I should be home before midnight. It's not even noon yet."

There was an audible sigh. "Yes, love, I do starve myself. I can't bear the thought of being without you and I'd rather go hungry than eat alone, if you must know the truth. Besides, I hate cooking for one. Do you know how long it takes to figure out a recipe for one person? These things serve families, not the single bachelor. And did you ever think that perhaps I might just enjoy your company a little bit? Hmm?"

She moved her fingers like a mouth to make fun of him. "Are you finished?" she asked and put her hand on the door. "If so, I'd like to get inside where it's warm and make my delivery so I can get back home. In case you didn't know, it's kind of snowing here." She opened the driver's door and hopped in. Her key was in the ignition and turned before the door shut.

"I'm never done, thank you very much. But for now, I'll put it on pause. Should have your notes done by the time you get back. There's not a lot to tell this time. If you think of anything else, let me know. I'll add it later." A soft click sounded in the background as he typed. "So we don't need containment for this one, right?" he asked.

She shook her head as if he could see her and said, "Not this time. No containment, no extras, just straight delivery. I actually like that better. Gets the money to my account that much faster," she chuckled. Warm air flowed freely from the vents as she removed her gloves. "I can feel my fingertips again. How nice," she mumbled. "Any way, I'm heading to Portland to make my delivery and I'll be home hopefully no later than ten. Sound good?"

"Works for me. See you soon, love," Linx answered.

"See ya later, Linx."

•   •   •

A black sedan idled in an empty parking lot as a long puff of steam trailed behind in the frosty grey air. The headlights of the Jeep slid along the side of the shiny paint job and stopped on the driver's window. As she shifted into park, Haydeez silently asked that this not take too long. In the middle of the day, the temperature still read only thirteen degrees. She was scared to think of what the wind chill was and tried to focus on the task at hand. With a sigh, she turned off the ignition and removed her key. Her subconscious told her the cold air had already begun to seep in and it would take over soon enough. She shoved her hands back into her fuzzy gloves and opened the door. Her uncovered face was greeted by a blast of icy air that almost took her breath away.

Behind her, the canine began to whimper again. She dropped her head and sighed. "Really? The sad doggy thing again? Please stop. I really can't handle that." With her jacket cinched tight, she opened the back door. The canine let out a howl as if to plead with her one last time and Haydeez flinched. She scooped it up and bumped the door closed quickly before she changed her mind.

"Ah, the Hoko. I see you had no trouble trapping it. Well done. Peter will be pleased," a man said as he stood beside the black sedan. "Any special instructions this time? I don't see any fancy lights or expensive gadgets holding it down." He chuckled.

Haydeez sighed. "Just keep it in the net. It won't cause any problems for you. Just put it on the back seat and make sure it stays wrapped up." She held her arms out, offering the dog to the man.

He laughed. "Back seat? This isn't the boss's pet. This is just some creature." He pressed a button and the trunk popped. "It goes back here," he said as he nodded to the opening. "No special treatment."

A pang of guilt pinched her right between the eyes. She tried to brush it aside as the man took the creature and dropped it into the trunk. It yelped and whimpered again as the trunk slammed shut. "I'll need that net back in one piece. I can always come get it from Peter if that's easier," Haydeez said.

"Until next time, Haydeez," he said with a smile and a tip of his hat. "Safe travels to you." His smile was unpleasant and unsettling as he opened his door and climbed into the driver's seat.

"I'll keep trying," she said. Haydeez just stood there and watched the sedan drive away. She could almost hear the dog whimper from the trunk. The feeling of guilt spread through her as the chill took the heat from her flesh. She shook her head and got back into the Jeep. With her finger to her ear, she said, "On my way." Her fingertips brushed over the GPS quickly as heat filled the interior.

Calculating route.

"Well, that didn't take too long at all did it?" he asked.

"Nope, I'll be home soon," she answered shortly.

"You alright?" he asked.

"Fine. I'll see you soon," she said and clicked off her earpiece.

Chapter 2

The front door slammed shut with a loud boom and vibrations that shook the house. Linx looked up, knife in hand, and waited for Haydeez. He watched as she stormed into the kitchen, almost ripped the door off the refrigerator, and then slammed it shut.

"Lasagna?" he asked tentatively as he held a plate out to her.

"It was a dog, just a simple dog. It thought I was playing with it. What could the Council possibly want with a dog?" She smacked her hand down. "A dog, Linx! It ran around, tongue hanging out, jumping from tree to tree." She rubbed her hands over her face. "It could've been a puppy and I shot it with lead dust." Her shoulders slumped. "Did I do the right thing?"

Linx put the plate down and wiped his hands on a towel. He walked around the island and put his arm around her shoulders. "If you beat yourself up every time you trap a creature, you'd be bruised and bloody every waking moment. Trust me, you don't want to beat yourself up. You hit really hard, I mean, *really* hard." He playfully shoved her. With a smile, he added, "Ready to eat? I know you're hungry. I could hear your stomach growling when you drove up."

Haydeez chuckled. "It better not have fish in it. You know I hate fish." She grabbed the plate and turned to leave the room.

"How do you know if you hate it until you try it, love? You don't do you?" he called after her. "You'd like it the way I cook it. You've liked everything else." He grabbed his plate and followed.

With a smirk, she answered, "You keep telling yourself that. If it helps you sleep at night..." A chime sounded from inside her pocket. She groaned. "Damn it." She placed her plate on the table and fished her phone out. "Hello?" She rolled her eyes. "Peter, always a pleasure. To what do I owe the honor of your call this evening?" She made a motion with her hand as she impatiently listened to the man on the other end of the call. "Your dog picked up my dog. They should be on their way to you right now." There was a pause. "Is my money in the account?" Another pause. "No, Peter. Of course I'm not trying to get you off the phone so I can sit down and eat something after being on the road for several hours doing a job for you. Why would you think such a thing?"

Linx chuckled and shook his head. He placed two glasses on the table and pulled a bottle of wine from a nearby rack. With his eyes on Haydeez, he pulled the cork and waited next to the table for her to finish the call.

An audible pop echoed through the dining room as Haydeez rolled her head back and forth. "I left it in a net, covered in lead dust. It should be fine. Speaking of my awesome toys, you owe me several UV lights from the last little bundle that I shipped out to you. They better not be damaged from mounting them to the inside of that trunk. Think you could have your lapdog send those back to me sometime soon? I use those a lot." She rubbed her neck and groaned. "Thanks, I'd like them back in one piece, same way you got them." She pinched the bridge of her nose. "Yeah, just ship it and I'll pick them up." She hung up the phone and looked at Linx.

He raised the bottle and smiled. "He always makes me want to drink."

Haydeez laughed and pulled out her chair. "Better fill that glass."

Chapter 3

The soft click of tiny shoes echoed through the halls of a children's hospital in Sacramento. A young girl about twelve walked happily from door to door in search of something. A middle aged nurse stopped the girl and asked, "Is there something I can help you with dear? You look lost. Are you looking for someone?"

The girl replied with a smile, "I was looking for a very special friend. Will you help me?" She asked politely.

The nurse held out her hand and said, "Of course, sweetheart. Whatever you need, I'll be happy to help."

With a giggle the girl took the nurse's hand. "Will you be my friend?" The child asked as she allowed the woman to guide her over to the nurses' station. The young girl was sweet as honey with a smile to match. She sat down in a desk chair and spun around with a giggle as she watched everything around her fly past. With an abrupt stop, she faced the nurse. "May I please have a drink? My throat is terribly dry."

"Sure, dear. Why don't you follow me and we'll pick out something from the snack closet. Then we'll find who you're looking for up here." The nurse smiled and reached out a hand again. "Just remember it's our little secret," she added with a wink.

The girl giggled again as she took the nurse's hand. "I won't tell if you don't tell." She hopped off the chair and skipped down the hall with the woman.

"My name is Maggie. What's yours?" the woman asked.

"My name is Eve. It is very nice to meet you, Maggie." A hint of gold flashed beneath her clothing. Her fingertips brushed her shirt as if to quiet something. "I am sure you will be able to help me today." Her tiny shoes clicked on the freshly waxed tile floor.

They stopped in front of a door and the nurse fished a set of keys out of her pocket. She unlocked the door and guided Eve inside. "What would you like, Eve?" she asked. "We have plenty to choose from. If you'd like, I think I can sneak a snack for you too."

Eve looked at Maggie and walked over to a cooler. She pulled out a bottle of juice. When she turned back around, a gold disk hung around her neck over her clothing. It sat quietly against the soft material of her shirt. The stone in the middle began to swirl. Eve spoke in a language Maggie could not understand. Her black curls fluttered with a breeze that came from nowhere.

Maggie looked on as fear crept into her face. "What are you doing, child? What do you want?" she asked as her voice wavered. As she moved towards the door, it slammed shut and locked. Maggie jumped back, tears in her eyes. "What do you want?" She asked again with a quiver in her voice.

The child giggled again. "I told you. I'm Eve, but most people call me Pandora. I just want the help you offered. You said you would be happy to help me and now I want to give you something for being so generous. It will help you to help me. It's a gift. I just know you'll like it." She bounced up and down and clapped her hands.

Tears streamed down Maggie's cheeks and trails of black appeared in her golden colored foundation. "What do you want? Are you going to kill me?" she asked in a whisper.

"Of course not, silly. How will you help me if you're dead?" A shadow began to spread out from the middle of the disk. Pandora watched with glee. "Look! It's your gift!" She cried out as the shadow took shape.

It shimmered and trembled as it flowed from the center. Once it was completely free, it stretched and shook itself like a dog. When it straightened, the shadow settled in front of Maggie for a moment. It took in all the details of the nurse's face, tasted her fear. Desire emanated from the shadow as it twisted and writhed in the air. It fed from the woman's raw terror until it practically burst.

Pandora watched with wide eyes as the shadow bulged from the feast. "You have made my friend very happy. It will enjoy being a part of you. Don't worry, it will not hurt for long." She rubbed her hands together and smiled. "The pain will end quickly."

The shadow swayed before Maggie's eyes. It trapped her in its gaze, like a mongoose with a cobra. Its eyes glowed red as it looked at the terrified nurse. Fangs formed in the creature's mouth. Several moments passed as the shadow played with its prey. Maggie's shoulders relaxed and her body slumped to the floor. The shadow took advantage and swept forward. In one fluid motion, it smothered her in the smoky depths of its body. It flowed into her eyes and ears as she gasped for her last breath.

Pandora squealed with delight. "You will have lots of fun here. There are many children all around and you've been trapped for so long. Feast, lamia. There are plenty more."

Maggie's body convulsed. Her mouth snapped open as a grunt escaped deep in her throat. Fangs forced their way out of her gums as her skin darkened and peeled. Maggie's heart pounded as it threatened to rip a hole in her chest. Her fingers stretched and claws protruded from the tips. As a spasm rocked her body, the claws struck the floor and tore holes into the cold tile.

Pandora stood by and watched with wide eyes, not in horror but in excitement. "Show yourself, lamia. It's time to indulge."

When the spasms slowed, the creature had fully taken control of Maggie's body and turned it into what it needed: flesh and blood strong enough to carry the spirit of the lamia. It slowly lifted itself off the floor. The areas of skin that had peeled away on her arms and legs shimmered like new snake skin, smooth and sleek.

Pandora opened the door. "Your meal awaits," she said as she waived the lamia out the door. They left the food closet and went down the hall in separate directions. The lamia burst into the rooms quickly and struck its prey.

With a smile on her lips and screams all around her, Pandora walked down the hall to the glowing exit sign. As the door closed behind her, silence flooded the stairwell.

Chapter 4

Haydeez woke to the sound of her phone as it vibrated on the nightstand. Her hand shot out from under the jumble of blankets and pillows and snatched up the phone. She pulled it back under and answered in a muffled voice. "This better be important." The mountain of bedding shifted as Haydeez sat up. "How many so far?" she asked as she brushed tangled strands of hair from her eyes.

She pushed back the thick comforter and swung her bare feet to the floor. "Any idea where it's headed?" she asked. "Do you want it alive?" She chuckled as the voice answered. "Didn't think so, but you know I have to ask first. I've got it. I'll call when it's done." She clicked the phone off and hopped off her bed into the fuzzy slippers below.

The purple silk pajamas fell into place as she walked across her bedroom and into the hallway. "Linx, time to get to work," she called down the hall. "Linx! You better be awake!" she yelled.

A loud thud sounded from a room down the hall followed by a groan. Linx mumbled incoherently and untangled himself from the mix of blankets and sheets. His hair stood straight out on the left side and was smashed flat on the right. He wiped the sleep from the corners of his eyes and stood up. "I'm awake! I'll be there in a minute!" he called back to Haydeez through the closed door.

After about fifteen minutes, they met in the kitchen. Haydeez looked fresh and wide-eyed, ready to get her day started. Linx, however, looked like he could use another day of sleep. Haydeez handed him a cup of coffee and said, "I hope you'll be more alert when I tell you what's out there right now." She took a sip and set down her cup.

Linx held up a finger to tell her to wait a moment and took a gulp of his coffee. As the hot liquid burned his tongue and slid down his throat, he squinted. After a moment, he took a deep breath and said, "Right, what's the problem today, love?"

Haydeez picked up her coffee cup and walked out of the kitchen. "Let's go see," she said over her shoulder.

They walked down the stairs to her work room in the basement and stopped at the first metal table. A laptop sat open with a file pulled up. "You've already looked it up?" Linx asked, surprised. "But we just woke up."

With a chuckle, Haydeez tilted the screen to read. "For some of us, it doesn't take as long to wake up and function. I put the coffee on, came down here, and looked up this latest creature right away. Didn't take long at all actually." She looked down at the screen and began to read. "Lamia: a vampiric demon who preys on children. Lamia are from Greek mythology. They take the form of a woman and devour the children of others. The atrocity of the act has deformed the creature who was once human. According to this, Lamia was actually the name of a woman. She was Zeus's mistress, or one of them I should say. He really did get around. Hera got pissed and killed all of Lamia's children which drove her nuts." So looked up and added, "So we're dealing with a creature that lost something important to her and is now taking it out on families that have never had anything to do with what happened. Why can't anyone ever just go after the one that screwed them over and then be done with it?"

"You wanted this to be easy, love? You're in the wrong line of work," Linx laughed. "So, how can we get rid of it? You said 'vampiric'. So, do we use the light?"

Haydeez took a sip of coffee. "Sounds like a plan to me. I'll bring some extras just in case but, if nothing else, that should slow it down a bit." She moved around the table to collect some items and throw them into her hunting bag. "Should be an easy trip. Do you mind hanging back with the animals?" she asked.

Linx clicked a few things on the laptop as he answered, "No problem. I've got some new snacks to share."

She rolled her eyes and zipped up the bag. "If he throws up, clean it up. Don't let him upstairs. Oh, and don't forget to feed him actual food." She began to head up the stairs. "I shouldn't be long once I find it."

Chapter 5

A set of automatic doors opened with a swish. The warm air from a high-powered heating unit spilled out onto the drop off in front of a hospital.

Haydeez pulled out her sunglasses as she made her way into the chilled air. "When they say nothing, they really don't mean 'nothing'. There were body parts and bones everywhere. Only parts missing were all the organs. This thing had a feast." She shivered. "It was like a rabid animal went on a feeding frenzy." She slid into the Jeep and cranked on the heater.

She chuckled as she added, "By the way, the CDC cred worked perfectly. Nobody really fights back when the CDC is checking on something. I'll have to use this one more often. I like the response."

"Who's a genius?" he laughed. "So, do you have any idea where to go from here?" Linx asked.

With a sigh, Haydeez said, "I follow the bodies."

· · ·

An eerie silence swept over the empty playground as Haydeez surveyed what was left of the carnage. Her stomach dropped at the thought of how many children will die because this thing was still free. She wondered how long it would take to stop it and how many more families would suffer. Her brain tried to focus on the task at hand. With her feet carefully placed in an area without blood, she stood in the middle of the playground and stared at the leftover body parts. There were not even enough pieces left to make one child.

The cold hid some of the smell but the odor of dead flesh still accosted her nostrils. She brushed it aside and tried to use other senses to take in the details. There were no sounds around her. The birds were gone, no cars roared past, and the other children who had survived were safe at home with their families. The caution tape flapped as another breeze floated around her.

Her eyes caught sight of something in the dirt and she made her way over to it. A lump caught in her throat as she attempted to swallow and took a deep breath. She touched a deep scratch as she knelt on a dry patch of ground. Slowly, her fingers brushed the crumbled dirt. Images and sounds immediately flashed through her brain. She heard the panicked screams and saw the flood of tears. The lamia growled and flowed over the children like a viper. The dark creature took bites from the children's bodies. It did not bother to kill the children first. It ate them while they were still alive the way a snake swallows a rabbit or a rat. It appeared that none managed to escape. "So much for survivors being safe at home with their families," she mumbled angrily.

Her heart raced as the images engulfed her brain. Her breath caught in her throat and sweat formed on her skin. She jerked her hand towards her chest and cradled it as if something had burned it. Tears rolled down her cheeks. Her body shook in sadness and anger. Everything in her wanted to yell at the top of her lungs and curse the creature for what it had done and will do before she finds it.

Unfortunately, the creature was already cursed and nothing she said would help the children who had lost their lives here. Her body shuddered and she wiped the tears away. She touched a finger to her ear and said, "This needs to stop now. You have no idea what these children felt. They were eaten alive. They were so scared. I..." She paused. It was one thing to go after an adult with the ability to defend itself but an innocent child, there was no reason for this. "We need to stop this. Who would want to destroy all these children? What do you gain by doing this?"

"I'm actually glad I don't know, love. If I did, it would mean I started thinking like one of them. Then I'd have you hunting me and I know I don't want that," Linx said. "We'll find it and stop it like we always do." He waited for her to say something. "Still with me?"

She responded with a heavy sigh. "I think it is headed west. Looks like the light isn't going to work. It attacked these kids during the day. I guess it doesn't care about the sunshine." She stood up and wiped the dirt from her hands. "Might take me a little longer than I thought. See if you can find anything else that can kill it. I'll call you back when I get on the road." She did not want to talk anymore. There was nothing to be said that was more important than the task at hand. This creature needed to be killed before it took another life.

She spun around to face the direction the lamia went in her vision and focused. The caution tape flapped again.

"I'm coming for you. Prepare yourself for the end." She took off for the Jeep, determined to make the kill before the next sunrise.

Chapter 6

The soft hum of a heater took the edge off the silence as a formidable man sat behind a large desk. His deep eyes fixed on another man that sat across from him. "How many years have you worked for me, Donny? Twelve? Thirteen?" he asked in a gravelly voice.

The man swallowed. "Fifteen years this spring, Stavros. I started as your accountant right after Easter services," he answered quickly.

"Why are you sweating, Donny? Is it too warm in here? Miko turn down the heat. I think Donny's a little uncomfortable." The heater immediately clicked off on the other side of the room. "There we go. Now, I have a little gift for you, Donny. After all your years of service," he said as he opened a drawer and pulled out a box. "For you, Donny." He tossed the box to the accountant.

Donny reached up and caught it in the air. With a hint of confusion in his eyes, he opened the box and pulled out a shiny gold pen. He picked it up in his right hand and tested the feel. His body visibly relaxed. "Thank you, Stavros," he said as he mimicked writing for a moment.

Donny admired the gift and smiled to himself. He was too busy to notice the slight nod from Stavros. Before he could see what happened, there was a thick hand on his neck and another on his left wrist. With a grunt he was forced forward. "What's going on Stavros?" he asked as his voice cracked.

A deep voice from behind his head said, "In the context of this meeting it would behoove you to address him as Mr. Campanos." Miko squeezed Donny's neck slightly.

"What happened, Mr. Campanos? Did I do something?"

Stavros leaned back in his chair and sighed. "You've been stealing from me, Donny. You don't steal from family. Family provides for each other, takes care of each other. I know you've been keeping two sets of books. Normally we would handle stealing in a more," Stavros paused as he pulled a gun from a drawer, placed it calmly on the desk, and continued, "permanent fashion."

Donny tried to shake his head but Miko had a grip on the accountant's spine. Tears began to well up. Miko squeezed Donny's wrist and moved his hand to a large metal paperweight. He shoved the man's hand down onto the dome and spread his fingers flat.

"I have been more than lenient with you and far beyond patient as I waited for my money to return to me. But it hasn't returned, has it, Donny?" Stavros asked.

Miko leaned into Donny's ear and calmly said, "Answer him."

"No, Mr. Campanos. It hasn't," Donny said with another grunt. Sweat glistened on his forehead and his breath came in heavy gasps.

Stavros removed a hammer from the same drawer and placed it on the desk next to the gun. "This is what will happen. My money will come back to me one way or another and today," he paused. In one swift movement, he picked up the hammer and raised it above the metal dome. "You are punished for what you did wrong."

Screams of agony intermingled with the sound of crunched bones and the occasional ting of metal on metal.

Donny's eyes began to roll back into his head.

"No, no, no, Donny. You don't get to pass out. You *will* stay awake for this." Stavros dipped his hand into a glass of water and splashed the dazed accountant in the face.

When the sound of crushed bones faded and only Donny's pleading whimper remained, Miko released his neck and wrist. Donny cradled his swollen mangled hand.

As a calm radiated from the large man, Stavros placed the gun and hammer back into the drawer. "Now, this is what you're going to do when you leave here. Miko will drive you to the hospital. When they ask you what happened, you will say that you were changing the tire on your car, the jack slipped, and the car crushed your hand." He took out a towel and cleaned the smears off his paperweight. "And if you decide to tell them anything different, well, Miko here helped you move in to your home, didn't he."

Donny whimpered again and nodded slightly. His entire body shook as he held the purple puffy blob that used to be his left hand.

"Good, it looks like we have an understanding. Now, you'll take a few days off to rest and I'll see you next week. You're not fired, of course. You have to get my money back to me somehow, right?" he asked with a smile and a chuckle. "You'll notice that I didn't hurt your right hand. I want you to be able to continue doing your job. After all, you are a great accountant and it takes time to find someone so good with numbers." He smiled again. "Miko, take him to the hospital. Make sure he gets some proper care."

Miko grabbed Donny and lifted him out of the chair. As he opened the door, a man stood on the other side poised to knock, a little girl at his side. "We're done, buddy, go on in," Miko said.

Stavros eyed the door. "What's going on?"

The man did not speak as they walked into the room. The young girl smiled. "Hello there, sir." She sat down in the chair that Donny had vacated. Her companion stared blankly ahead. "My name is Eve and I have a proposition for you. By the way, I love your work. Much more creative than pulling a trigger or smashing a knee cap." She giggled.

Stavros glanced back and forth between Eve and the man who brought her. "I didn't think it was cookie season yet. So that means you're selling services and I like my women legal."

Eve giggled again. "That must be the only legal you like in your life but that's really not why I'm here. How would you like to expand your empire? Create fear in your enemies that hasn't been seen since Greece and Rome battled?" She pulled the gold disk from under her sweater. It pulsed and glowed. "I can give you that power."

Stavros turned his chair away from Eve and said, "Listen here, girlie. I don't need tips from a kid on how to run my business. My associate can show you out now." He waived a hand over his shoulder.

Eve scoffed. "I don't think you understand what I'm offering here." A sly smile spread across her lips. "Aren't you tired of the Greek mafia being on the low end of the pole? Aren't you sick of the Italians and Russians making fun of your family? Don't you want to be more than just a joke? Greeks used to be feared. They were a force to be revered. They belong on top and I can bring you back to the pinnacle of their glory."

His shoulders tightened. With his face still turned away from the girl, he said, "I think you need to go."

She spoke quickly and the gold disk glowed and hummed. "Why don't I give you a creature so powerful that it took a god to stop it? Your family would work together to create an empire so great that your enemies would fall to their knees in fear of your wrath." A low growl rumbled throughout the room followed by the hiss of a snake. "Your gift is ready, sir. All I want is for you to keep someone busy while I take care of some of my own business. What do you think? Will you help me?" she asked excitedly.

Stavros looked around the room. "What's that noise?" He saw nothing at first. Then a heaping mass of shadow spread out in front of the girl. "What the hell is that?" he shouted as he jumped from his chair. It fell to the floor with a thump.

Eve smiled. "That's your gift. Do not worry, it's not here to harm you. It is here to help you achieve your most secret goals. Your deepest desires can be yours if you just say yes. You would need your family, of course, to complete the transfer." She sat still in her chair as she awaited his answer.

The mist pulsed and billowed in front of Stavros. "My family? Why do you need my family?"

With a giggle, Eve said, "Because there's three, silly. You would take up the head, your wife would be the tail, and your son would be nestled in the middle. Together, you could strike fear into anyone who crossed you... and so many more. They will bow before your greatness. Just picture it. You would trample all who opposed you." She breathed heavily. "You know that is what you want, deep down in your heart. Take it. Say yes." Her eyes sparkled eagerly.

Stavros stared at the mist for several long moments, mesmerized by it. With his eyes still focused on the shadow before him, he pressed a button on his phone and said, "Bring my wife and son down to my office immediately. It's urgent."

Eve smiled. "I'm so glad you see the benefits I offer you."

Chapter 7

A knock broke the silence as a man patiently waited outside the private office of Stavros Campanos.

"Enter," Stavros said from behind the closed door.

Light sliced into the darkened room. Heat visibly poured into the hallway like a watery mirage on a desert road. The man removed his jacket before he stepped into the illuminated rectangle on the floor.

"Mr. Osbourne, welcome. Please come in and take a seat," Stavros said calmly, a slight growl to his voice.

When the door opened further, all he could see was an arm that extended from the shadows and swept into the room to welcome him to an open chair. "Please make yourself comfortable. You have been accepted into this office," Miko said from behind the door.

Steve Osbourne walked into the room, jacket over his arm, and sat casually in the plush chair. He ran a hand through his black hair. It took a few moments to acclimate himself to the darkness. As his eyes began to adjust, he could make out some objects but could not see Mr. Campanos. As he breathed, a musky scent entered his nostrils. It reminded him of his trips to the zoo as a child.

The window had been covered by what appeared to be papers. It looked as if something had taken a chunk from the corner of the desk and several lines streaked across the front. The only thing that made sense to Steve was that a large animal had made the marks but he brushed it off. After all, this was the middle of the city. He decided that the heat had distorted his vision and his mind played tricks on him. "What can I do for you on this lovely evening, Mr. Campanos?" he asked. He leaned back in the chair and rested his arm on the low back.

There was a rustle in the shadows followed by a low growl and a hiss. "Mr. Osbourne, we are looking to hire you today for a more... personal matter." His voice sounded deeper with a gravel quality to it. He continued. "An associate needs a young woman out of the way for some time and you will be the one to do it."

Steve nodded. "I understand. Take care of her like the usual. Absolutely, Mr. Campanos. Accident or purposeful hit?"

There was a hiss followed by a deep growl. "No, we must make this perfectly and completely clear. You are not to harm her. That was specific to the instructions. She needs to be kept occupied. Take her attention away from her job until I tell you otherwise. No maltreatment needs to come to her. Our associate would still like to utilize her in the future."

Steve continued to nod as he listened to the instructions and took in every detail.

"This job is out of the ordinary for you," he growled. "There's no death or destruction involved. But we trust that you will continue your same level of professionalism that we have come to expect while you are in our employ."

"Expect nothing less, Mr. Campanos. That's why you come to me. I'll keep this..." he paused. "What's her name?"

With another low growl, Stavros answered, "Haydeez Blackhawk. She's also a hunter but she specializes in 'out of the ordinary' bounties."

Steve chuckled. "Well, that's quite an unusual name. I'll be sure to keep her busy."

"Yes, well she's definitely not ordinary. But then again you'll find that out when you meet her." There was a rustle and a scrape in the shadows as Stavros moved. "Miko will give you her location. You'll have an expense account to cover any costs you incur during our employ. Make sure you keep her busy until we contact you with further instructions. It's our understanding that she's going after someone who's killing children. Not exactly something we abide. We truly hope she finds whatever it is soon." Another scrape followed as he shifted again. "Miko," he growled. "Please get Mr. Osbourne the information he needs."

"Yes, sir, Mr. Campanos," Miko answered from the shadows. His broad frame came into the light. He lifted a large hand as he motioned Steve out the door. "Follow me. Mr. Campanos will be in contact when he no longer needs your services."

As the door closed and all light disappeared from the room, silence flooded the office. A low growl and a hiss began. The snap of jaws followed. "Our end is done, little girl. You had better keep up yours."

Chapter 8

Haydeez crept through the shadows of a tiny wooded area behind a baseball field. The sounds of a game flowed into the empty spaces between the trees. Parents cheered for their children. The crack of a bat echoed and more cheers and laughter followed.

All of her focus was on the area around the field. She sniffed the air and listened. She had tracked the lamia and discovered that this was the first place that would have enough children to attract the creature's attention. Her moccasins crunched the dead leaves with each step.

"Haydeez, I think I found something," Linx whispered into her ear.

"Go," Haydeez responded, her words barely a whisper.

"I hope you brought your fancy knife with you. That'll be the easiest and least messy way to kill it. Otherwise, you'll need to cover it in rosemary and salt and then set it on fire," Linx answered. "So, either you're prepping it for a fancy dinner or you just stab it. Your choice, love."

She inhaled the cold air and held it for a moment as it opened up her lungs. "I know it's here. It's not getting away this time," she said as she exhaled.

The crack of twigs made her freeze in place. "I heard something," she breathed. She moved towards the sound. It took great care for her to step only on the balls of her feet to make the least amount of noise as possible.

She saw movement ahead and flattened herself against a tree. Her lithe frame slid around the trunk quietly and flowed into the shadows as if she were a part of them. With her eyes focused on the figure, she moved from tree to tree until she was a few feet away. "Who the hell are you?" she blurted.

The figure spun around. He reached for his weapon as the heel of Haydeez's foot connected with his temple.

"What the…" was all he managed to get out before he fell to the ground with a thump. He groaned for a moment. Then, his eyes rolled back and he lay on the cold ground unconscious.

"Lightweight," Haydeez mumbled and shook her head in disgust.

• • •

When the man regained consciousness, he sat with his back against a tree trunk and a gun, his gun, pointed at his face. "Not how I planned on spending my evening but at least the view is nice."

"Who the hell are you and why should I let you live?" Haydeez said as she held the gun steady in one hand. "If I don't like your answer, you don't see another sunrise."

He chuckled. "I heard you were different. My name's Steve. I'm chasing a bounty." He cleared his throat. "Is it ok if I move? I've got a bit of a lump on my head and I'd like to make sure there's no blood."

"There's blood," she blurted. "Last name."

"Great. Another scar," he mumbled sarcastically. "Osbourne. Do you always interrogate fellow hunters? You know we're on the same side right?" he asked with a smile.

She stood still for a moment, ready to fire. Then, without a word, she pulled back the gun, made sure the round was no longer chambered, and clicked the safety. "You check out." She turned away from him but held the gun at her side. "She's still here somewhere. I just hope amateur hour didn't scare off the prize." She scanned the area.

"Did you just call me an amateur?" he asked. With a hand on the back of his head, he checked for the blood. "Listen up, sweetheart, I'm a lot of things but an amateur is not one of them." He moved to get up but noticed she had turned to face him again.

"No, you heard right," she mumbled, her eyes fixed on Steve. "How about you listen up, kindergarten? If you heard that I'm 'different' then you heard I don't play well with other kids. Stay off my playground. You better hope you're hunting a different bounty. Otherwise, you'll end up going home sad and alone."

Steve stood up to face Haydeez. He was taller than her by almost a head. With a smirk, he asked, "So, if I'm after someone else, that means you'll come home with me?"

Haydeez stepped back and shook her head. "What? Where would you get an idea like that? I never said that! I said you'd be sad and alone, like, you won't get paid because you won't have a bounty to collect anymore. Why would you even think I would want to go anywhere with you?" She waved her hand at him as if to dismiss him. "That may work with bimbos but I actually have standards."

He crossed his arms and asked, "And what are those standards? I'm curious now what it takes to grab your attention." He smirked again.

"Someone who isn't you is a good start," she answered. She spun on her heel and started to walk away.

"How about giving back my gun?" he called after her.

There was an audible click and his empty gun landed at his feet. "Might want to learn to be more specific," she said over her shoulder.

"That was totally flirting, love," Linx said in her ear.

"Whatever. I wasn't flirting. He was obnoxious. He's lucky I didn't kill him to save the world the trouble of having to deal with him. Besides I don't want a loaded gun at my back," she whispered. "Now, maybe, I can get back to work." She scanned the area again.

"Actually I meant that he was flirting with you but it's nice to know your conscience is feeling a bit guilty this evening." After an extended pause, Linx asked, "He's not a bad looking guy if you like that sort of thing."

Haydeez rolled her eyes. "And what sort of thing is that?" she asked in a whisper.

"The tall, good looking, dark, mysterious type," Linx said. "I've got his picture right here. He looks like one of those bad-boy types. That's your thing, right? I mean, pompous rich guy is definitely not your type and adorable tech guy doesn't catch your fancy. So, it's gotta be the bad boys, right?" He laughed.

"Ok, that's enough chit-chat for the evening. I'll call you when I'm done," she said and clicked the earpiece off. She took a deep breath and moved around another tree quietly.

The sound of leaves caused her to freeze. She searched the shadows for the lamia or any sign that it was here. She felt something brush against her hand. In one swift movement, she grabbed and twisted whatever it was and turned to see what touched her.

"Wow, you're fast," Steve said with a grunt. "Mind if I tag along?" he asked. He gripped the arm she had trapped. His knees planted firmly on the ground. "I'd love to see what makes you so different."

Haydeez groaned and threw her head back. She continued to twist his wrist as she said, "Please leave me alone. If you cause my bounty to get away, I'll take you in instead." She dropped his arm. "This may be a joke to you, but this is a job for me. How about you go over there and let me finish my work?" She crossed her arms and waited for him to decide.

Steve stood up, dusted off his knees, and ran a hand through his hair. "If that's what it'll take to get you to talk to me, we'll do it your way." He turned and walked closer to the tree line. "I'll wait over here for you."

Haydeez groaned and turned back around to focus on the hunt again. "This has been a very trying night," she mumbled to herself.

A strange breeze whispered ahead. She froze and watched as a dark shadow weaved between the trees. It looked like a tall woman with the walk of someone who clearly was not afraid. In spite of the darkness, there was a glossy shimmer to her body. Her hips swayed as she walked towards the tree line in the distance.

Haydeez quietly moved a little closer. She noticed the shimmer was actually the skin and the sway of the hips was in reality a reptilian body. She reached down to her thigh and slid a shiny dagger from its sheath. With a flick of her fingers, it flipped and laid against her wrist. She moved faster to reach the lamia before it crossed the tree line.

When she was about ten feet away, she stepped on a branch in an attempt to grab the creature's attention. The snap was louder than intended but the end result was still achieved.

The creature spun around faster than something that size should move. It hissed. "You're not a child. What do you want? It's time for me to feast." It swayed like a cobra dancing to a flute.

"Whoa, you're really not pretty up close. I mean from far away you looked like a beautiful woman but up close, yikes. Have you seen yourself?

You're a mess! Makes killing you so much easier," Haydeez said. She crouched down and waited for the creature to move.

"You cannot kill me, female. I am eternal. It is my destiny to take the lives of children everywhere. You are an adult and as such, you are not worth my efforts." The creature inhaled deeply. "You have not bred. This is a waste of my time." It turned to head back to the tree line.

Haydeez took advantage of the lamia's cockiness. She pounced on the creature and slashed at the scaly body. "Wait. I haven't bred. What is that supposed to mean?"

The creature cried out in pain as steam rose from the wound. "What have you done, female?" It twisted and reached back to touch the now burnt opening. The scales peeled away to expose skin. "What is that cursed thing?" it shrieked. "Don't touch me!" It flailed around until Haydeez lost her grip and dropped to the ground in a crouch.

"Guess your kind doesn't like being blessed." She smiled. "Let's see how long it takes to strip you down to just bones." She sprang up and slashed again. A chunk of the creature's chest opened up. "How long do you think you can take the pain?"

It howled in agony. With claws extended, the creature reached out and tried to swipe at Haydeez. It wheezed as the flesh sizzled and bubbled. Behind the steam, exposed bone began to show.

Haydeez chuckled. "Well, that didn't take long." She noticed how slow the creature had become since the first gash. "I really thought this was going to be more difficult. I had hoped you'd put up more of a fight. I mean, aren't you supposed to be something big and scary? I could've sent Linx out here to get you." She struck the creature again, this time in the throat. "You're nothing. At least those kids out there have nothing else to worry about. They can play their game and worry about school but they never have to be scared of you. You'll never kill again." With one last thrust, she struck the creature in the head with the knife.

There was another shriek. The parents in the stands cheered at the same moment. Nobody heard the creature cry out in anguish. Haydeez watched as the lamia's body sizzled and writhed and melted into the cold ground. There was no sympathy when the last bits of skin and muscle boiled off the creature's bones.

When silence settled all around her, all that was left was someone Haydeez did not recognize. She just stood there with a blood covered knife and watched. She figured that this was the nurse from the hospital. When they find the body, they would figure the nurse went crazy, close the case, and no more kids will die because of it. It was a shame for that innocent woman to take the blame for that horrible act but there was nothing that she could really do about that part.

"What happened? I heard a scream," Steve said. He moved around a tree and the body came into view. He stopped abruptly. "Is that your bounty?"

She sighed. "Sometimes it just doesn't go the way you'd hope," she responded. "But at least she can't hurt anymore kids." She sighed again. "Those kids over there will never know how close they came to being killed by this thing. I'm glad they'll never know. It's one less nightmare they'll have to have."

Steve looked between Haydeez and the body several times before he spoke. "So this is what they meant by 'different'. Not exactly what I expected but still not the worst thing I could think of I suppose." He inhaled deeply and let out a sigh. "Well, I'm glad that wasn't my bounty because you were right. I would not be happy right now. Hey, do you want to get some coffee? I'm sure you could use it right now."

Haydeez chuckled. "It's not like this is my first kill. Most of them don't exactly want to be caught." She cocked her head to the side and knelt down next to the body. "Damn. I was wondering when you'd show up again," she mumbled. Her fingers brushed against a brand on the nurse's neck. "Looks like we'll be meeting again soon."

"What was that?" Steve asked. "I didn't hear you."

"Nothing. I think I'll pass on the coffee. I don't fall for the 'wanna get some coffee' ploy. If you're looking for someone to hop into bed with, I'm sure there's plenty of willing girls at a bar somewhere nearby but I'm not one of them." She used the nurse's clothes to wipe off her knife, stood up, and brushed off her jeans. "Besides, I have a long drive home tonight. Not really interested in putting it off." She started to walk away.

Steve turned and caught up with her. "Ok, so you don't want coffee. How about food? I'm sure you need to eat something. My treat. What do you think?"

She rolled her eyes. "I've got some calls to make. Are you going to leave me alone anytime soon?"

With a smile, he said, "Not until you say 'yes'."

She groaned. "Fine. As long as you're paying, I think I can spare a few minutes."

Chapter 9

"The knife worked great. Actually it worked better than I thought it would. She was done after a few hits," she said. With a chuckle she added, "Wouldn't it be nice if everything was this easy?"

Linx laughed. "Don't get used to it, love. Besides, I'd be out of a job if it was."

"By the way, this one had the mark. Looks like Pandora is making her next move. If we're correct, we need to start looking for Greek creatures this time," Haydeez said. "Kind of fitting for her since she's Greek and all. So, keep your eyes out for anything that falls under Greek mythology and give me a call if you find anything before I get back." She paused. "I'm grabbing something to eat and then I'll be on my way."

Linx was quiet for a few moments. Then he said, "Ok, just please be careful, love."

"Always. I'll let you know when I'm on my way." She hung up and prepared to make the next call.

There was a knock on her window. She held up a finger. "It's me. It's done," she said. "I can wait." After a few moments, she said, "Great. Thanks for the business. Call me if you need anything else." She opened the door and hung up the phone. "Ok, all done. Let's go."

•   •   •

Haydeez cleared her throat. "Look, I get what you're trying to do but I'm not interested in anything like that right now. I have a lot going on and the last thing I need is someone fawning over me and trying to impress me." She took a sip of her drink. "It always feels like I have someone I have to answer to and I like it when I'm only answering to myself."

Steve laughed. "That's not even close to what I was asking. I have to bring someone to this party and the only women I ever meet end up in handcuffs by the end of our first conversation. Not exactly 'fancy party' ladies if you know what I mean. Besides, having the best looking woman there would be a groove for me," he said with a smile.

"Wow, that's what you've resorted to?" she rolled her eyes. "Being here is one thing. It's public. If I go missing, they'll know you were the last one with me. But you want me to go to a stranger's home with a stranger. I can take care of myself and all but I'm not an idiot."

"So, you've never wanted to go to one of Piven's annual parties? I've been told that if you ever have the chance to see one, take it. He's quite the showman and only the best of the best are invited," he added with a grin.

Haydeez shook her head. "Wait. You're saying you've got an official invite to a Cornelius Piven party? How did you get that? Are you sure it's official? How do I know it's not a fake and you're not just setting me up?" she asked, more confused with every word he spoke.

Steve laughed. "I guess I'm just that special." He paused. "Actually, someone I used to work with asked me if I wanted to go and then got me on the guest list. It happened pretty quickly. I said yes but I didn't really expect to get the invite. Now I'm stuck looking for my plus one. So," he paused again. "What do you think?"

She took a deep breath and sighed. Reluctantly, she said, "Fine. I'll be your plus one. Any chance to get inside his house and see his collection is worth putting up with someone like you. I've heard he has some amazing pieces." She took another sip. "When is it?" she asked.

He pulled out an ornate invitation with a fingerprint scanner. "It's in three days in the Olympic Mountains. Fancy dress." He turned the invitation to face her. "Mind scanning your finger? The invite needs to be personalized."

Haydeez looked at the details. It looked real to her but she had never been invited and, thus, had never seen one before now.

Cornelius Piven was a reclusive man every day of the year, except when he threw one of his parties. He liked to show off his money and all the weird things he collected over the years. There was always a curiosity in Haydeez that poked her subconscious. Now she had the chance to see it for real.

"This is a real invitation, right? If you're screwing with me, just know that I can take you down without you even realizing what happened," she said without as much as a smile.

He cleared his throat. "Well, I can always find someone else if you think it's a trick. You really have no reason to believe me. I mean, we just met. I'm surprised you came with me to have food. But, I won't force you." He pulled back the screen.

"Just give it to me," she responded as she held out her hand impatiently. She placed her thumb on the screen and watched the red light turn to green. "Anything else I have to do?" she asked.

"Nope, you're good. I'll pick you up but you'll have to tell me where you live." He grinned.

Haydeez groaned. "Just remember, if you come to my home with bad intentions, your body will never be found. Understand?" she asked. When he nodded in agreement, she provided her address. "This is only for the party. I don't want to see you hanging around in the bushes, stalking me."

Steve laughed. "If I'm on your property after the party, I guarantee you won't consider it stalking," he said with a wink.

Haydeez rolled her eyes. "You're awfully sure of yourself."

He smiled. "I've never been wrong about my abilities."

Chapter 10

On a tiny island in the south of Greece, two separate golden mists floated through the air in front of Pandora. They awaited their orders. A young woman stood in awe, her eyes wide as they took in the entire scene.

Pandora spoke to the glowing clouds and they began to take shape. One formed what looked like a large fox. The other took a more human form and flowed over to the woman. It quickly entered her lungs and flooded her body with its power. She eagerly accepted the mist and smiled as it filled her chest. She let out a small yelp of joy as her body began to change.

The other mist encircled a stray dog that Pandora had trapped. The dog growled and snapped its jaws at the cloud. As its teeth clamped down on nothing, the mist flowed between the teeth and down the dog's throat. It cried out in pain. The animal's body convulsed as it, too, transformed.

When the cries faded and silence filled the empty building, Pandora giggled. Before her stood a woman covered in shimmering snake-like scales. Her hair was pulled up into a bun with ringlets that hung around her face. Strands of gold were interwoven throughout her hair. She wore a silken dress in hunter green that resembled something the ancients would've worn. Her eyes were the same emerald as her dress, however, they were more closely related to those of a serpent. There was a slight sway to her body as she breathed. "Greetings," she hissed.

"Well hello," Pandora responded cheerfully. "Are you ready to help? Your host body was very eager to participate in any activity I had planned. It's always welcome when someone needs no convincing. The process is smoother and less painful for the spirits."

The woman inspected her hands and arms. She ran her fingertips over her arms and down to her stomach. As she stopped, the scales melded into her flesh and left a sheen that gave off a glittery quality. "Hmm, this should allow me to walk amongst humans without questions. So, what would you like me to do for you, child of Hephaestus?"

Pandora smiled. "I'll explain in a moment." She turned to the creature that was formerly a dog. "Great fox, I need you to go on a hunt. Your job is to follow your instincts. There are many children out there. Just do what you do and make sure none are left alive."

The Teumessian Fox nodded its large head in understanding and turned to leave. Its body was the size of a male lion. The fluffy tail swished as it disappeared into the darkness.

Pandora turned back to face the woman. "Now for your task, Euryale. I need for you to retrieve an item for me. It holds great power and it will be an integral part of my plan. Once you've retrieved it and brought it to me, you will be free to do whatever you choose."

Euryale flashed her fangs. "Seems simple enough. What item are you in search of, child?"

"I need a Phenix egg. There is a human across the ocean. He does not quite realize what he has in his possession. His home is filled with artifacts that contain magic but he believes them to be pretty objects. He has the egg on display in his home. He will be hosting a party but you will need to be on someone's arm. I have located a man who will get you in, however, once inside, you will need to locate the egg on your own."

Euryale's skin shimmered as she moved. "And who is this human? Does he need to remain alive?"

"The human does not matter. I need the egg. Once you have it, get out as quickly as possible. I cannot have the safety of the egg risked." Pandora eyed Euryale. She looked into the gorgon's eyes without fear. "And his name is Cornelius Piven."

Euryale stared back. "Then, I will retrieve the egg and return quickly. I do not enjoy being under the control of another, especially one so young and inexperienced. This man who I am accompanying, do you require his services further?"

Pandora huffed. "Let me make this clear. The only thing that matters is the egg. I don't care about anyone or anything else. Just get it and get out."

"Consider it finished," Euryale hissed. "I must ask one last thing." She paused for a moment. "Why do you not just enter this party yourself and take what you seek? It would seem easier to just do for yourself instead of seeking the employ of others."

With a sigh, Pandora answered. "There are reasons. With all the items he keeps in his home, there is too much mystical energy flowing around. It is too much for this human body to handle." She smiled and added, "I also have other matters to attend to and, in order to keep my plan on schedule, I must seek the assistance of others. Now, if there are no other questions," she paused and turned on her heel. She called out and a man walked out of the darkness. "This is your escort. He will get you into the event but he knows nothing of the egg and will not be able to help you find it."

The man did not speak. He just held out an electronic pad towards Euryale.

"Please touch the screen with your finger to accept the invitation. Then you will be able to enter," Pandora said.

Euryale touched the screen. It beeped and turned green. Pandora smiled. "You're ready to go."

Chapter 11

Linx ran after Haydeez. "Are you sure you want to do this? It doesn't sound safe to me." He caught up to her and added, "Besides, you barely know him. Why would you go with him?"

Haydeez laughed. "I've always wanted to go to a Piven party. Do you know how hard it is to get invited to one of those? I don't care how he got the invite. I don't care that I have to go with him. I want to go." She stopped and faced Linx. "This is a once in a lifetime chance for me to see this collection. I can't even imagine what he's got in there. People say he doesn't even know what he has. They say he just collects pieces but doesn't realize what they're worth. I think he's got some powerful stuff there and doesn't understand the damage he can do." She made her way up the stairs. "Now, I have to get dressed."

Linx rolled his eyes. "Then let me come with you. It would be better if you had backup."

"No, for a few reasons. You have to be invited and you weren't. I don't need backup for a party. And then there's the issue of having you hover over me because there's another boy showing me any kind of interest," she said with a smirk. "Are you scared I'll replace you?"

He shrugged his shoulders. "Sometimes, but that's not the point. What do you even know about him aside from what I was able to pull up?" Linx huffed. "Everything could be made up. Or even worse, he could be using you." Linx crossed his arms.

Haydeez stopped. "Are you afraid he'll be a repeat of the past? I mean, it's not like I'm marrying him. In all honesty, I'm using him to get into this party. Does that help?"

Linx thought for a moment and said, "Actually it does help. Just please be careful and keep your ear piece on at all times, just in case you need anything."

"I think I can handle that. It shouldn't clash with my dress." She laughed. "Keep an eye out. He'll probably be at the gate soon."

·   ·   ·

A buzz on the call box broke the silence. Linx sighed and pressed the button to answer. "Yeah? Who is it?" He had to answer the door but she never said he had to be nice about it.

"Steve Osbourne. Haydeez is expecting me," he answered.

There was a buzz as Linx pressed the gate button and sighed again. "Here we go," he mumbled.

After a few minutes, he heard the rumble of an expensive engine and a knock. When he opened the door, his shoulders slumped. The only thought that crossed his mind was whether or not this guy's actual last name was Bond. However, the only thing to come out of his mouth was, "Bollocks."

Steve laughed. "You must be the voice in her head." He stuck out his hand. "I'm Steve."

Linx reluctantly reached out and shook the outstretched hand. "Linx," he said. "She'll be ready soon," he added and motioned into the house.

"You're British. Not what I expected when she told me about you," Steve said.

Linx ignored him and closed the door. They made their way into the warmth of the living room and sat down on the plush couches. A long silence filled the air with only the crackle of the fire to fill it.

After what seemed like hours, Steve asked, "So, how long have you known her?"

Linx leaned back and said, "Many years. We've been partners for a long time. I live here." He blatantly tried to slip that in as a way to mark his territory.

Steve lifted an eyebrow and smiled. "I see." They sat for a few more moments in silence before he asked another question. "What's with the bike? Does it work or is it just a fancy piece of art?" he nodded toward the Harley.

"Belonged to someone she hates. She keeps it there as a reminder of what he put her through and to not trust pretty boys anymore," Linx answered. "She likes trophies of her conquests."

Steve laughed again. "Interesting." He put his arm across the back of the couch. "I get the feeling I'm stepping on toes here but I was under the impression that she was single. Which is it?"

With a sigh, Linx said, "I don't speak for her. I don't make decisions for her, and no, we're not together. I just like to make sure that anyone who sets foot in this house can be trusted. Not to mention, I need to make sure that my best friend is safe. With her line of work, it's important to make sure strangers don't take advantage of her."

"So, you're like an overprotective brother. I can understand that," Steve said. "I'm just here to take her to a party. I promise I'll have her home by curfew," he joked.

"A bit more than a brother, mate," Linx said through gritted teeth. Before he could say anymore, he heard a door close upstairs. From the landing Haydeez called down, "I'm ready."

The two men stood up and turned to the staircase. Haydeez stood at the top in a long purple satin dress. It hung off her body like a waterfall and still managed to cling when necessary. Her shoulders were bare except for the cascade of golden ringlets. As she took a step, a long line exposed her leg almost to the hip. She held a purse small enough to be inconspicuous but large enough to hold a weapon or two. "I see you managed to keep yourself from killing him, Linx," she said with a smile. "I'm impressed."

Linx stood completely dumbfounded. His heart raced and he could not form words correctly. The only thing he could do was stare. He saw Haydeez every day for many years now, whether it was in the heat of battle, as she drank her morning coffee, or just seated in front of the fire. He knew how he felt about her but seeing her this way, for someone else, nearly broke his heart.

"So you're not always carrying a gun and running through the woods. Good to know," Steve said with a smile.

"No, and sometimes I get my nails done and go to the beauty parlor too," Haydeez responded with a roll of her eyes. "Let's get going. I don't want to spend my whole night talking to you. I'm sure there will be much more interesting people in attendance," she added with a forced smile.

Steve laughed. "A sense of humor. How refreshing." He held out his arm. "We had better get on the road if we're going to be on time for the party."

She took his arm and Linx flinched. He handed her a coat and then followed them out the front door to what was waiting outside. In his mind, Linx shouted, "Oh come on! Can't he just have something wrong with him?"

Steve pulled out the keys to a McLaren and clicked a button. The doors popped open as they approached.

Haydeez turned to Linx and said, "See you in the morning." She then slid into the front seat and melted into the soft leather.

Steve closed her door and headed to the driver's seat. With a nod and a smile, he said, "Good night, buddy."

The engine roared to life. Linx was left standing in a cloud of snow as the McLaren sped down the driveway. "Brilliant," he mumbled.

Chapter 12

"Are you sure this car is safe in the snow?" Haydeez asked as they wound their way through the Olympic Mountains.

Steve laughed. "You're safe. Not to worry." He glanced at her and added, "I wouldn't open the door if I thought you were in any kind of danger."

It was Haydeez's turn to laugh. "I'm not worried for my safety. I'm more concerned that someone as soft as you might get damaged if something happens."

"Soft? I wouldn't really say..." he started to respond. "Oh, we're here." They pulled up to an iron gate with a speaker box. Once they identified themselves and the gates opened, they were on the way up a long drive much like the one on Haydeez's property.

A large mansion spread out in front of them. Valets parked expensive cars in the distance. Multi-colored lights lined the drive up to the door. The outside had been tastefully decorated for the holidays. The guests quickly entered the warmth of the house to escape the bite of the winter air. Men stood at the door and scanned fingerprints to allow the partygoers to enter.

Haydeez studied the entryway. Wreaths and the smell of cinnamon welcomed everyone. She held in her excitement and masked it with forced pleasantries. "There's a lot more people than I expected. Makes me wonder how he chooses his guest list. You would think he would only want a few people at a time," she said. "Kind of makes me feel a little less special." She chuckled.

"I wouldn't say that. I'd say you're pretty special," Steve chimed in without hesitation.

Haydeez rolled her eyes and said, "Right. You're coming off a little desperate. Compliments don't unlock my bedroom door, Steve. Just remember that."

A young woman took her coat and handed her a ticket. "Feel free to mingle throughout the house. Mr. Piven will be down to greet everyone shortly," she said with a smile.

Steve laughed. "Is that what you still think I'm doing? Wow. Who disappointed you and made you hate kindness?" He shook his head. "For destroying you for anyone else, that guy needs to be shot."

"Don't really want to talk about that right now," Haydeez answered. "Not the place. Not the time."

They walked through the house. Haydeez was not really interested in speaking to the other guests. She had her eyes set on the multitude of mystical pieces on display. The vibrations called to her like a song she remembered from childhood. Each piece had its own melody and they sang a beautiful chorus. She rested her hand on a pedestal as she admired a redish-gold crown made of cobras. It looked Egyptian. The plaque read: *The golden crown of Wadjet – believed to control the serpents of Egypt. When the chant is spoken correctly, the wearer can call upon the serpents to do his/her bidding.* A chill danced between her shoulder blades and she shuddered.

"The real deal," she whispered under her breath.

"Are you cold?" Steve asked.

"Just trying to warm up a bit. Still feeling the chill from outside," she lied. "I'll be fine."

He moved to put his arm around her. Before he could touch her, she stepped forward and asked, "Oh, what's that?" With a look of utter dejection, Steve sighed and followed her.

Men in tuxedos and women in long gowns maneuvered between pedestals. They stopped and casually read the plaques beneath sculptures, pictures, or scale models of inventions. The guests commented on how interesting it would be if they were real and not just stories.

The sounds of laughter and chatter dulled in her ears as she looked around the main hall. Paintings dotted the walls. She soaked in every brush stroke as she admired an original DaVinci amongst several scale models of the artist's inventions. Her fingers brushed over the miniature crossbow, small enough to mount on a wrist brace and fire from the back of her hand. The details put into the model were amazing. It appeared to be perfect in every aspect. "I bet this actually works," she mumbled to herself. "I could really use one of these."

Steve looked at the wall and saw nothing but a beautiful painting. *Salvator Mundi* stared back at him quietly. He hardly noticed as Haydeez began to walk away.

Slowly, she walked along the wall. Her fingers ran along the wallpaper until she stopped at a sealed shadow box. Perfectly preserved beneath the glass was a small branch. "Yggdrasil," Haydeez said. "This is supposedly from the World Tree." Her eyes glistened and sparkled. "Can you even imagine what that could mean if this is real?" she asked Steve. "This is amazing." She turned and began to walk away again.

"How do you know so much about this stuff?" Steve asked as he followed her.

"Everything is always trying to kill me. Knowledge is power, Steve," she answered without hesitation. She stopped in front of a pedestal. "You've got to be kidding me," she blurted and then covered her mouth quickly. "A Golden Apple of Discord?" she whispered. "This is amazing," she said again.

They stopped in front of a glass case that displayed a dagger. She read the plaque. "The dagger of beniice. Beautiful. I didn't know this actually existed. It's said to have brought the change in seasons when used by the tribe's shaman." She sighed. "I'd love to see it in action," she mumbled to herself. Her eyes glittered as she studied every inch of the unusual piece.

She had never seen a stone dagger before and this one was particularly interesting. It appeared as if someone had imbedded chunks of gold and silver in the dagger. A hum filled her brain as she continued her gaze. "I would love to just hold it for a moment," she said to herself.

Before another thought could cross her mind, a male voice from behind pulled her back to the party. "Perhaps that can be arranged one day, Ms. Blackhawk."

She turned quickly. In front of Haydeez stood an older man with flecks of white hair. She could not contain her surprise as he reached out a hand to introduce himself. "Cornelius Piven. It's quite a pleasure. When I heard you were attending this evening, I made sure I would have plenty of time to greet you personally," he said. Cornelius stood out in a room full of well-dressed men and women. He wore beige cargo pants and a brightly colored Hawaiian shirt over a green t-shirt. His sandals completed the picture and spoke volumes for the kind of person he was.

"Wow, I can't believe you know who I am," she answered. She took his hand and shook. "I've hoped to have the chance to attend one of your parties. I've heard your collection is amazing. So far, it hasn't disappointed." She smiled.

"Well, as I stated, I may be able to arrange a private viewing. I'd love to get another expert's opinion on some items I've recently acquired," he said with a smile of his own.

Her stomach fluttered. "So, you *do* know how much your collection is actually worth." She paused. "I would love to have a chance to examine some of these pieces more closely. That would be amazing. I'm honored that you consider me an expert. Not that I'm upset or anything, but how do you know who I am?" she asked.

Cornelius chuckled. "We travel in the 'same circles', my dear. I've heard your name mentioned on more than one occasion and I have to admit that I've been truly curious to see if what I've heard is true."

Steve's eyes shot back and forth like he was at a tennis match. "There's so much more that I need to learn about you. Are you some kind of history buff or something?" he asked.

Haydeez chuckled. "Something like that. I do a lot of research into different mythologies. I like stuff that's weird and unexplainable." She shared a knowing look with the eccentric billionaire.

"And I feel out of the loop here. Would either of you like a drink?" he asked.

Before they could answer, a crash silenced the party.

Chapter 13

A scream pierced the night. At the top of the stairs, a woman stood in fear before she turned and raced down. She looked over her shoulder every step of the way. As she neared the bottom of the stairway, her foot slipped and she tumbled the last couple of feet.

"No!" she shouted. "No, I need to get out of here." She scrambled to her feet and ran through a small crowd of people towards the door.

Haydeez blocked her path and asked, "What happened?"

The woman put her hands up and tried to shove past Haydeez. "Let me go! She's coming to kill me. I have to get out of here."

Haydeez grabbed the woman by the shoulders. "Who is coming? Who wants to kill you?" she shouted.

"I don't know but she said she'll kill me!" the woman yelled again. She shook herself free and raced out the front door.

A switch flipped inside her brain and Haydeez turned towards the stairs. "Mr. Piven, do you screen your guests before the party?"

"Of course, this is my home. I don't want criminals stepping through the door," he answered. "And it's not like someone can just break in here. Have you seen my security? No, you haven't because they're that good." He looked upstairs. "Any idea who it might be?"

She began to walk to the stairs. "Has to be a guest, right? Time to find out. You might want to stay here, Mr. Piven. Don't want anything to happen to you."

With Steve in tow, they made their way up the stairs. Cornelius remained on the first floor to calm his guests.

•   •   •

Haydeez pulled a small gun from her purse. She placed her purse on a pedestal with a curved vase etched in ruby chips. "Oh, pretty," she mumbled. "That would look nice in my dining room." She shook her head and focused back on the hallway. Muffled thumps led her to a cracked door four rooms down on the right. She motioned over her shoulder for Steve to stay behind her and quietly pushed the door open.

When she looked in the room, broken furniture littered the floor. A tall woman stood with her back to the door. In the shadow of the small table lamp, her skin shimmered like wet scales but the floor was completely dry. She was dressed like the other guests which probably put her on the list.

Haydeez motioned to Steve that there was only one person. She slowly moved into the room with her back against the wall. "Something I can help you find?" she asked.

The woman turned with a casual demeanor. "No, I believe I have found what I came for tonight. However, if you prevent me from leaving, just know that this will be your last night alive." Her voice carried a condescending tone.

Haydeez sighed. "If I had a dollar... Ok then, let's get this over with so I can get back to the party. Are we talking weapons or fist fight?" She held the gun steady.

With a laugh, the woman answered, "Weapons? Darling, my body is my weapon." By the end of her sentence, her dress had already begun to press into her skin, to be replaced by shiny snake scales. They trailed down her body and led into a thick tail. From her shoulders down to her ankles, her whole body swayed slightly as she slowly slithered across the room towards Haydeez. She held a large oval shaped object. "Not to worry though, this will be quick and painful."

Steve stood outside the room in awe. He saw the woman transform and could not speak. His skin drained of all its color. If Haydeez needed help, he would be absolutely useless. He watched in confusion as she held her gun steady, unsure of why she was not fazed by any of it.

"Wow, that's a handy trick but I think I'll stick to this," she said as she motioned to her gun. "Now put that back before a blow a hole in that shiny body of yours."

The creature laughed. "Euryale does not take orders from a filthy mutt such as you. Your blood is muddy, you disgusting half breed. You are therefore beneath me. Step aside, mongrel, so I can make my delivery." She slithered and swayed. "You should stay out of my business, pup. You're well beyond your league."

Haydeez scoffed. "Never been called a mutt before, but damn. Not cool. That was a whole bunch of insults in that little speech of yours. Why all the hate? Did I buy a purse made from your babies or something? I think that almost hurt my feelings." She cocked her gun. "Almost. Now, I don't mean to be rude, but, well, no I do mean to be rude. Drop it or die. Last chance."

Euryale slithered closer. "Go ahead. Find out how big of a mistake you're making. Pull the trigger, little cur."

"Done," Haydeez said. She pulled the trigger but the bullet did not quite react properly. It bounced off Euryale's scales and ricocheted into the wall. "Really? Come on." Her shoulders dropped and she lowered her weapon. "It's never easy." She sighed. "Fists it is I guess." She took a few quick steps and swung.

Euryale chuckled. "You cannot beat me. You are not my better, not even an equal." She snapped her tail but Haydeez leapt into the air. Her tail hit the side table and shattered it to splinters. She swung back around and struck out again. Her tail banged into the wall with a loud thump.

Haydeez raced up to take another swing. Euryale snapped her tail and caught Haydeez on the ankle. The hunter flew forward and smacked her face into the floor. She groaned. Before she could roll over, Euryale pinned Haydeez to the floor beneath the full weight of her thick tail. With a loud grunt, she twisted her body and tried to free herself. Her eyes caught sight of something all too familiar. On the side of Euryale's ample body was Pandora's brand. "Great," she mumbled. "Should've known you were one of hers."

"Hey!" Steve yelled from the doorway. He came into the room and began to fire his gun futilely. "Leave her alone whatever you are." His gun clicked empty. "Damn it." He froze for a moment as Euryale focused on him.

Anger filled her eyes. "You are a mosquito. Allow me to crush you like one," she hissed. Her body swayed and weaved around the debris on the floor. "Perhaps I'll eat you when I'm finished." She flicked her tongue. Her body jerked and moved backwards. With confusion apparent on her face, she turned her head. "You."

Haydeez gripped Euryale's tale and pulled. The movement looked awkward with her hair done up and her silk dress. Her muscles tightened as she dragged the creature. "Naughty, naughty. People are not on the menu tonight," she grunted. "You're done, lady. I am so sick of you and we only just met. Time to go away." With a loud groan she yanked Euryale by the tail and flung her out the window.

After a loud crash, Euryale's body flew from the upstairs window. She yelled. "I will find you again, mutt!" Her body twisted and landed in the snow with a soft thump.

Steve ran up behind Haydeez and looked down. They watched as the snow shifted and Euryale's body rolled out. It twitched and flipped back onto the belly. She brushed the snow from her face. With a glance over her shoulder, she showed off her prize and slithered away quickly. She had managed to grab the egg.

Haydeez smashed her hand on the windowsill and yelled in frustration. "I know something bad is going to come from this. We need to talk to Piven." She turned and started to walk from the room.

Steve scoffed. "Care to explain what just happened," he called after her.

She turned around. "Not sure but I will definitely find out soon. I only hope I can get that egg back before it gets used for something terrible."

.   .   .

Cornelius poured a cup of tea. "I had my theories but I never thought I might actually be correct." All the guests had left and he sat in his study with Haydeez and Steve. Security had verified all the fingerprints as the guests left and they had figured out who had let her into the party. At this point, it did not really matter, but he made sure that person would never appear on another guest list again.

He fixed his tea and took a sip. His Hawaiian shirt was completely out of place in the room full of priceless antiques. His whole body was out of place, until he spoke. "As I said, I've wanted to meet you for some time but I wasn't certain how to find you, or if you were even real for that matter.

There are so many stories about you and what you do. I wasn't sure if they were true or just exaggerations to be honest. Now that I see you here, I can tell that you're not ordinary. After what you did up there, I think they underestimated your capabilities. Actually, I believe that you may know what just about every item in my home is and whether or not they are real. Am I correct?" he asked.

Haydeez eyed him for moment and then said, "That's quite possible. I would love to take a look but I really need to figure out tonight first. Do you know why this thing would want that egg? I'm still trying to figure out what it was."

"Gorgon," Linx chimed in her ear. "Euryale was one of the sisters. Medusa is the most well-known but there were more. Euryale was supposedly the most ruthless. Pandora probably promised her freedom in exchange for that egg." He cleared his throat. "Are you sure you're alright?"

"Yeah, stop worrying. So that was a gorgon then," she said as she quickly changed the subject. "Why didn't she turn me to stone?" Haydeez asked. She swept her spoon through the hot liquid and tapped the side of the cup.

"They aren't all the same. They do different things. Medusa's thing was turning people to stone. Euryale was an assassin. She was brutal." He paused. "Are you drinking tea?"

Haydeez took sip. "Nope," she lied with a smirk.

Linx scoffed. "Yes, you are. You told me you hated tea. I'm going out to get some before you get home and you're drinking it. I'm done with your bitter coffee. You can drink tea with him but when I ask," he grumbled.

Haydeez chuckled and cleared her throat. "So, if this one doesn't turn things to stone, how do we beat it? Bullets don't work."

Cornelius cleared his throat. "I don't think that's our biggest problem. That egg belonged to a phenix. It's meant to bring eternal life through rebirth. There are many stories surrounding those eggs but just know that they are terribly rare." He took a long sip. "I don't know what she's planning on using it for but when a gorgon is involved, it can't be good for anyone else."

"Wait, phenix? Don't you mean phoenix?" Haydeez asked.

Cornelius answered. "Some mythology call it a phoenix. Old blood knows it as phenix. Many legends say that seeing one meant there would be a great disaster followed by an even greater rebirth... a cleansing, if you will."

Steve just watched. He looked confused but nobody seemed to notice. He tried to understand. Nothing made sense. He had so many questions but did not want to seem like everything was new. It took every ounce of strength in his body to not jump up and scream.

"She called me a mutt and said my blood was muddy. Why does everyone keep saying stuff like that to me?" she asked. "Do I give off an aura or something? It's really starting to bother me."

Cornelius ignored her question and stood. "I wonder if I still have that book." He walked to a bookcase and began to scan the spines. Shelf after shelf of leather bound books stood before him. Each one was just as old as the last, perhaps older in some cases. After a few moments, he pulled a worn tome gently from its home and carefully opened it. He quietly flipped through until he found what he needed. "I heard stories about that egg. While others believe in the whole disaster and rebirth thing, according to ancient Greek stories, the egg is meant to join the first man and woman in an eternal bond. They are meant to be born apart and find each other over and over until the end of time. The egg draws them together at the end of their lives. Once together, they die hand in hand and the cycle begins again." He sat back down. "I can't imagine why she would need it."

"What happens if it's broken? Can she kill one of them and end the cycle?" Linx asked.

"Good question. If it's broken does the the cycle end?" Haydeez looked at Steve. "Any ideas?"

Steve blinked a few times. "Well, I suppose if one of them dies, then the whole thing ends. But that would mean that the first couple ceases to exist. What does that mean for the rest of us?" He tried to sound like he was part of everything.

"If Pandora wants the egg, it means the end of man. Not sure how but," she paused. "All I know is that's her end game."

Everyone sat for what seemed like hours, but was really only a few minutes. "I hate to add to the storm but we've got another problem," Linx said.

"What?" Haydeez asked. Cornelius and Steve turned to face her as they could not hear Linx in her earpiece.

"There's another thing out there. I've been tracking it. I'm not sure what it is but, it's going after kids like the other thing." He sighed. "It's eating them, love. Everyone thinks it's a wild animal but there's too many dead and it's too widespread. I thought the lamia was bad but this thing, it takes a chunk out here and there and leaves the rest to rot. It kills and eats and moves on to the next. It mauls them. It never eats the faces. It's like it wants everyone to see the terror. It needs to be stopped, love. It doesn't seem to be getting full."

Haydeez tried to process the information and just sat for a moment. A thoughtful look crossed her face. "So now we've got more issues than we can handle. We've got to find that egg but I can't sit by while those children are killed." A heavy sigh passed her lips. "So, which one can be ignored?"

Chapter 14

The buzz of the phone woke Miko from a sound sleep. His boss wanted information and grew more restless every day. "This is Miko," he answered with a yawn. He glanced at the clock. The numbers four and ten glowed red and silently mocked him as he tried to sound professional. Miko fell back on his pillow with a grunt. "But you've been keeping her busy otherwise, right?" he asked. With a sigh he added, "I will let Mr. Campanos know. We will be in contact if your job duties change." The call disconnected before the other person could respond. "No time like now to deliver the news," he mumbled to himself.

•   •   •

A chair crashed against the wall no more than a foot from where Miko stood. He did not flinch. Not a word escaped his lips.

There was a growl and a low rumble from across the room. "Why would she have me send them to that man's house knowing that what she wanted was there? She wanted that woman out of the way and yet..." He growled again. "What was the point of that?" he yelled.

"I'm sure that witch had her reasons," a female voice hissed. "She seemed very sure of herself." A hint of irritation snuck out between her words.

Stavros growled again. "We agreed that this would be the best thing for this family. You can try to hide your annoyance but I can see inside your head now. Our son has accepted his place. Perhaps you need to learn from the men. I am in control. You are just along for the ride."

Miko noticed a change in Stavros. He seemed to lose his temper faster and became more chauvinistic. Miko was not afraid. The problem was that his boss had begun to lose himself in this creature. With every action, he left another piece of his humanity behind. There was no telling how long he would last but Miko did not want to be on his radar when he finally snapped. He never thought to leave Stavros for any reason, but there was always a first time for everything.

There was a hiss followed by a loud snap. "Don't talk to me like one of your lackeys. I'm your wife. I deserve more respect!" she yelled.

"If I didn't need you in this body, I would kill you myself," he roared.

"Should I wait outside, Mr. Campanos?" Miko asked.

A large creature moved forward into the light. It had the hind legs of a goat and the forelegs of a lion. It was covered in a golden brown fur. Instead of a head, the torso of a man sprouted from the ample shoulders of the lion. Strong arms crossed over the bare chest. A thick set of horns curled out of a full mane of bronze hair. Two pairs of eyes stared at Miko as a cavernous voice answered, "No, it would do her well to see what real loyalty looks like."

The head of a serpent swayed over his shoulder and hissed. "Loyalty. Useless," the serpent spat. "It never truly lasts."

Stavros kept two of his eyes focused on Miko while the other two glared at the serpent. His muscles bunched as his arm swung out and struck her. His wife cried out in pain as her body recoiled. "Loyalty lasts to a dying breath. Love just dies."

Chapter 15

"Can I take the bike?" Linx asked with a smirk.

Haydeez stared back with a look of derision. "The fact that you asked me that says you don't really know me as well as you think."

Linx chuckled. "I stepped away before I asked didn't I?" He closed his laptop and added, "You will be keeping contact with me this time, right? I have to tell you where she's going anyway. How else will you swoop in and do your hero thing?"

"My hero thing? You mean my job?" Haydeez chuckled. "Yeah, I'll keep in contact. Once you've got a location, let me know right away. Do not go after the egg yourself. You're not prepared for that."

Linx looked at Haydeez, a fake pout on his face. "Not prepared? You underestimate me, love." He chuckled. "I know better than to steal your thunder."

Steve walked down the stairs. "Are you ready?" he asked. "Can't find that thing if we don't start looking for it."

With a furrow in his brow, Linx asked, "You're going too?"

"He's helping me look for the fox. An extra hand will be helpful when I'm trying to kill this thing," Haydeez answered.

Linx scoffed. "Since when do you need help killing anything? You took down that golem on your own not too long ago." He paused. "Wait, did he spend the night?" He glared at Steve who only smiled in response.

"I'm not going to answer that, and you seem to forget who stabbed the Alpha while he was busy hovering over my bloody body," she responded.

With a wistful look in his eyes, Linx mumbled. "Right, I was pretty awesome. Wait, that means I can totally handle myself. Maybe I'll just grab the egg if I see it. Seems silly to have you come all the way out there just for that. We don't even know where she is by now. She could be far away and it might take days for you to get there. By the time you do, she might be gone. Sounds like more of a hassle to me," Linx joked.

Haydeez rolled her eyes. "Use that scale 1 found in the mess she left behind to track her. Don't go after them. Just follow. Nothing else." She stopped. "And maybe take some pictures. 1 need something to put in my notebook for when 1 take her down." She looked at Steve. "1 like to keep notes when 1 beat something just in case 1 come across the same thing in the future," she said with a smile. "1 call it my hunter's journal."

"Interesting. Mind if 1 take a look at it one day? Sounds like a good read," Steve said. His calm voice hid all the questions he wanted to ask. *Am 1 dreaming this? What are we going after? Why am 1 still here? What could possibly be in that book? Do 1 really want to know what's in there?* Then, a thought crossed his mind that scared him more than anything. *Those noises 1 heard in Mr. Campanos's office... was that him? Was he one of them? Oh god, has he been one all along? How do you hide something like that?* "I'll be upstairs," he said quickly. As he walked up the stairs, he shuddered. "What am 1 getting into?" he mumbled.

•   •   •

The jeep rumbled down the highway. Haydeez watched as nothing but trees and pavement sped passed her window. The sun dipped down below the tree line and stained the sky cotton candy pink. She glanced in the seat next to her. Steve stared out the side window. "We need food," she said loudly.

His body jerked and he smacked his head on the window. "Damn it!" He rubbed his forehead. "What did you have in mind?"

"Something to keep me awake. 1 need protein," she scanned the signs on the side of the road.

He cleared his throat. "1..."

"Stop before you start. Continue that sentence and I'll leave you at the next exit," she said quickly.

Steve laughed. "Ok, ok, you win. Any idea how long before we get to this fox thing?"

"According to the reports, the last kill was about 20 miles from here but if 1 don't eat soon, 1 can't be held accountable for what 1 will do to anyone around me," she said as she slowed down and pulled off at the exit. She touched her ear and said, "We're stopping. Let me know if you find anything new."

Linx sat on the side of the road with a laptop on the passenger's seat. He read the news story to see if it pertained to either hunt. "Nope, must be something else if adults were attacked. Moving on." He scrolled through a few more stories and decided that nothing new had popped up yet.

A blue light silently flashed on a handheld device on the dashboard. He turned back to the road, shifted into gear, and made his way down the highway again. "I see you leaving your trail behind, crazy snake lady. Not to worry. I won't let you get away." He glanced at the blue light and continued on his way.

As he drove, he could not help but let his mind wander. Unfortunately, it went to a place where Haydeez was alone with another man. He groaned. "Normally I'm fine with splitting up. We get everything done faster. But why did you have to take him with you? It's not like you can't find this thing on your own, and kill it yourself for that matter." He sighed. "Not my lady, not my place."

He continued to argue with himself as the car quietly raced down the highway.

Chapter 16

Linx pulled off to the side of the road. The blue dot blinked rapidly as he shut off the engine. He grabbed a camera from the seat and left the car without a sound. There was no movement in the area. In fact, everything seemed to stand still at that moment. It was like the calm of the island in Ireland in the middle of the storm. Something felt off but he had to take a look around.

He crept through the shadows of twilight as they stretched out around him. The soft blue blip was his only indication that the egg was near. He steadied his breath and strained his ears for a noise, a voice, anything to say that he was close.

He crouched low to the ground as the blip flashed violently. If the light was bigger it could have been mistaken for a strobe light in a club. Then, he finally heard something.

A gentle breeze carried a conversation his way. It sounded as if two women were in the middle of a heated discussion. His logical assumption was that it was Euryale and Pandora. He stepped lightly to avoid the crunch sound he normally made when he walked through dead leaves.

"I have done what you asked, child. Now I am free to do as I please. Our accord is complete," Euryale stated.

"You are correct, gorgon. As you have fulfilled your part of our agreement, you are free to wreak as much havoc as you please. I no longer require your services," Pandora responded.

Linx poked his head around the tree and saw Pandora with a large egg in her hands. His breath caught in his throat. He did not want to move.

Pandora snapped her fingers. "Done. You've been released. You're no longer tethered to my needs." She smiled. "Have fun, serpent. It would appear that you have some prey nearby," she added as she turned.

Euryale whipped her head around and flicked her tongue. She tasted the air, unaware of this prey Pandora spoke of, and angered that she had missed it. The slightest breeze touched the tip of her tongue. Her skin began to shimmer as scales appeared and her body transformed into that of a snake. "Human," she whispered.

"Aw, bollocks," Linx said. He jumped up from his spot and ran. "Really? Eaten by a snake lady? I don't want to die like this." He pulled out his phone and dialed. "Pick up, pick up, pick up. Ah, there you are, love," he huffed. "Just so you know, I found the egg."

"Why do you sound like that? What did you do?" Haydeez asked.

Linx grunted as he jumped over a root. "Honestly? It's my fault that creepy snake lady could taste me in the air?" He heard branches crunch behind him. "She's going to eat me you know."

"I like the taste of meat filled with adrenaline. It's much sweeter," Euryale hissed. "Keep running."

"How far away did I park?" he mumbled to himself. "I'm actually quite gamey. You don't want to eat me," he shouted over his shoulder. "Anyway," he huffed again. "I just wanted to share what I found. Gotta run, love. Bye." He clicked off the phone before Haydeez could answer and dropped it back into his pocket. "Am I running in circles or something? Bloody hell."

He heard branches snap on his left and then on the right. He could not tell where she was. Real fear began to set in. A root stuck out a little too high and Linx caught his foot. With a grunt and a thump he landed on his stomach.

Euryale laughed. "You allow your fear to consume you, human. It will be your undoing." She slithered over his leg and pressed it into the ground. "Interesting. You share a familiar scent." She paused as she flicked her tongue again. "I wonder if her mud has affected your flavor."

Linx felt her body tense as she prepared to strike. He wiggled his hand free, twisted his arm around, and struck out blindly with a small shiny blade. It sparkled as it struck her. As her body recoiled, he took that moment to flip over and pull himself to his feet. Tiny drops of dark blood dripped from the blade and soaked into the ground. He put his back to a tree and held the dagger in front of himself, ready to make a last stand if he needed.

"Did she tell you that would harm me?" Euryale asked. "She really did little to damage me. I am surprised that she was able to find something that could."

Linx scoffed. "I figured it out on my own. I'm more capable than you realize. I killed an immortal not too long ago," he said with pride. "I wouldn't get too cocky if I were you."

Euryale laughed. "Pride tastes bitter but I will suffer the flavor to end you." She hissed and swayed. Her tongue flicked as she opened her jaws. With her body tensed, she threw herself forward to attack.

Linx used all the strength he had and leapt to one side. His foot caught on her tooth and he fell to the ground with a grunt. "That arm still hurts sometimes," he groaned. He flipped himself over in time to see Euryale prepare to strike again. He thrust his dagger into her tail with all his strength.

"Puny human!" she shouted as blood dripped from her wound. "Your flesh is mine!"

Linx jumped to his feet and shook his head. The trees seemed to sway for a moment and he saw his car nearby. "Where did you come from?" he mumbled. He noticed Euryale was too busy with her wound. So, he took that moment to sprint for his car. He did not bother to look back. If she was close, he did not want to know. He grabbed the handle and threw open the door. In seconds, his shaky fingers fumbled with the keys but managed to get the engine started. He shifted gears and slammed the pedal to the floor. Dirt and dead leaves flew up behind him as his car spun around and left the trees in the rear view mirror.

Out of fear and habit, mostly fear, he slammed the automatic door lock button, just in case. "No egg and almost got myself killed. Yeah, she'll have a field day with this one," he mumbled to himself again. "Time to make a phone call," he sighed.

Chapter 17

"He hung up on me. What the hell?" Haydeez said as she looked at her phone.

Steve chuckled. "I take it you don't get rejected often."

She threw him a hateful look and answered. "It's not rejection. I'm sure there's a reason." She hopped into the driver's seat and mumbled, "There better be a reason."

Steve chuckled again. "So, how much longer?" he asked as he attempted to change the subject.

Haydeez started the engine. "We're off the highway now. It shouldn't be too much longer. Once we find it, we kill it." She checked her scanner and found the tiny light as it silently flashed on the screen. "I see you," she mumbled and headed towards the light.

•   •   •   •

"We're close. We'll go on foot from here," she said.

Steve eyed the screen and asked, "Are you sure that thing works? I mean, how can it track one specific fox?"

Haydeez laughed. "I followed an immortal Loup Garou with this and never once got lost. Yeah, I'm sure it works." She shook her head. "Let's go."

She pulled her bow and quiver from the back of the jeep and strapped everything in place. She paused and cocked her head. "Do you hear that?" she whispered. "I hear crying." Her skin rose in goosebumps and she gasped. "Someone is still alive. Run! We have to find them now!" She took off into an open field and headed for the tree line. "Move it! We have to find them now!" Her voice carried through the air. She had wanted to surprise the creature, until she realized it was in the middle of a meal.

Steve spun around and watched as Haydeez took off faster than a normal person. "Hey! Don't lose me!" he shouted after her.

Haydeez reached the tree line and did not stop. She dodged trees and roots. It was easy with all the leaves gone and many branches dried on the ground. She followed the cries for help. The fear in their tiny voices carried in the cold air. She had no idea how many were there but she knew she would do everything she could to save them.

The light flashed faster and she saw movement ahead. She tucked the device into her coat and removed her bow.

A large dead trunk spread across the ground ahead. It had cleared an opening in the trees. A small child huddled as far as he could between the trunk and the ground. His body shook so violently that Haydeez could see it before she was next to him. She crunched some leaves to get his attention and motioned for him to come to her.

The boy looked up, tears streamed down his face mixed with dirt and crushed leaves. He shook his head so fast he almost knocked himself out on the tree trunk.

Haydeez showed him her bow and nodded at him. She motioned again as Steve skidded to a halt behind her.

"What do we have? What do I do?" he asked. He looked over her shoulder and saw the boy. His breath caught in his throat and he could feel a lump form. "I'll get him, you get the fox," he whispered.

"Grab him and run as fast as you can back the way you came. Get him to the jeep. I'll be right behind you," she said calmly. She began to move to the right before he could answer.

Steve nodded in agreement, even though Haydeez was already gone, and moved quietly towards the boy. He crouched down and kept his eyes on the boy. Steve motioned for the boy to keep focused on him as he moved slowly and silently. His body was low to the ground as he did a weird crab walk. He watched Haydeez from the corner of his eye until she was lost amongst the trees.

The boy sobbed quietly as he waited for the stranger to come to him. His body continued to shake violently but he kept his eyes on Steve until he finally crouched right in front of him.

"We're going to get you home now, ok? I need you to trust me, ok? Can you do that?" Steve asked quietly.

The boy nodded quickly and threw his arms around Steve. As soon as the boy had a hold, Steve jumped up, spun around and ran. He held the boy tightly and just ran. Trees and dead branches flew past him. The boy let out huge sigh and began to sob loudly.

"You're safe now. We'll get you home soon," Steve said. "You'll be ok now, buddy."

The child squeezed Steve tighter and just let every emotion loose. Tears rolled quickly down his already soaked cheeks onto Steve's shoulder. "Why? Why? Why?" he screamed.

• • • •

Haydeez listened to the creature crunch its meal. Her stomach protested as she pictured a child being ripped apart. She pushed back the coffee and diner food and forced herself forward. With an arrow notched, she stepped quietly around a large oak tree.

A mass of flesh and fur towered over what was left of a child. Her body began to shake in anger. "No more!" she yelled. "That's your last meal."

The creature raised its head and a low rumble began deep in its belly. It moved a paw over the child and brushed it aside. It bounced away like a rag doll.

Haydeez released the arrow without hesitation. It struck the creature between the ribs.

A howl shook the trees and dropped loose branches to the ground. Haydeez had to jump to avoid being pinned by a rotted limb. "Good. I'm glad that hurt," she mumbled. "Time to die." She pulled out another arrow and fired.

The fox shook its head and charged. The arrow struck a muscle as it bulged in the creature's leg, but it did not slow. It remained focused on Haydeez and ignored the pain.

She spun around and ran for the nearest low branch and leapt. She caught the branch and hoisted herself up. As she tried to steady herself, the creature followed her and leapt up to the branch.

Unfortunately for the creature, the arrow that protruded from its side prevented a full extension of its body. It fell short and rolled on the ground. It whimpered in pain and stood up. With a growl, it watched Haydeez and circled the tree. The image of the creature brought to mind a panther or a lioness as it hunted.

"Told you it was your last meal," she taunted. With one foot on the branch and the other where the branch met the trunk, she pulled out another arrow and steadied her aim. She released the breath she had held and fired.

The creature leapt up and caught the arrow in the throat. It tried to growl but only a gurgle escaped. It pawed at the shaft in a feeble attempt to pull it out. Blood spilled from the wound as the creature fell to the ground.

Haydeez jumped down from the branch and walked over to where the creature rolled in agony on the ground. She lifted her foot and pushed the shaft further into the creature. "Instinct or not, I will not allow children to be hurt." She forced the arrow all the way in until it popped out the back.

It began to twitch and convulse on the ground. Blood pooled around its head and spread so fast that Haydeez had to step back or end up in the middle of the puddle.

After several minutes, the twitches stopped and the creature was still. A slight breeze caused the empty branches to creek and groan.

Haydeez listened as she scanned the area. Deep inside she had a bad feeling that nobody else was alive.

At that moment, she heard a rustle and a tiny sob. She raced to the sound as her heart beat quickly. A little girl sat huddled into a ball against the exposed roots of an oak tree. She hugged herself and rocked as sobs shook her body.

Haydeez dropped to her knees and threw her bow to the ground as she crawled to the girl. Blood splatter covered her back and her legs. "Is any of this yours?" she asked.

The girl fell back and tried to scramble away until she saw that a woman sat before her. Then, in one fast moment, the girl had wrapped herself around Haydeez and clung to her. "It's gone. You're going to be alright," Haydeez said. "It's all gone."

● ● ●

Steve watched the tree line for signs of Haydeez. He held the boy as they sat in the jeep and waited. The child had finally calmed down and, shortly after the tears had stopped, he closed his eyes and fell asleep. So, Steve sat in the passenger seat with a boy sound asleep in his arms, and waited for someone who may or may not come out of those trees.

After the howl he heard, everything went from 'just a walk in the park' to 'nightmares do come true'. He glanced at his phone several times a minute. "Come on, Haydeez. Don't leave me out here alone," he mumbled. "I have no clue what I'm doing here."

Fear of the unknown had turned into the desire to protect someone he had only recently met. What started out as a job, had turned into something he wanted to pursue on a personal level. He was terrified of whatever was out there in that forest. He had no idea what to expect, but when he watched Haydeez work, something inside changed. The mixture of respect and desire bubbled into a dangerous cocktail.

Steve noticed his fingers as they tapped on his knee. He had to make a conscious effort to stop. A heavy sigh escaped his lips. He pulled his seat forward and placed the boy in the back seat, careful not to wake him. With his arms crossed, he stood and waited impatiently for Haydeez to appear.

Pink polka dots bopped up and down in the tree line. Haydeez walked into the field with the little girl wrapped tightly in her arms. She moved her hand long enough to give the thumbs up and resumed her grip. The girl sobbed quietly.

Steve let out a grunt and took off at a run. He cleared the small field quickly and skidded to a halt in front of Haydeez. "Finally," he said. "I thought something had happened to you."

Haydeez eyed him with a pained look and said, "No big deal. Just a wild animal. Takes more than that to knock me down." She let out a strained laugh and pushed around him to the jeep. Her body was stiff and she walked with purpose.

She moved to place the girl on the back seat but the child protested. "It's ok. I'm just putting you in the back seat. We're going to take you somewhere safe now," she whispered.

The girl eased her grip and slid onto the seat. She wiped dirt and tears from her face and pulled her knees up to her chest. As she placed her head on her knees, her eyes closed.

Haydeez let out a sigh. "There were only two left," she whispered. "I don't even know how many it took." She rubbed her hands over her face and groaned. "Why is she doing this?"

Steve placed his hands on her shoulders and turned her around. "You can't do everything. Bad things are going to happen that you can't fix," he said. He wrapped her in a hug.

She put her head on his shoulder and sighed again. "I know that. Doesn't change the fact that kids died because I was too slow."

Steve laughed. "Too slow? I've never seen anyone move like you in my life. If anything, I was slowing you down." He paused and pulled back slightly to look at her face. "There's nothing else you could've done. The point is: you stopped it. What's done can't be changed but you made sure that thing can't do it again. Plus, you saved those two," he motioned to the kids fast asleep in the back of the jeep. "So, I'd call it a win and get those kids home."

Haydeez looked at Steve with a bit of sadness in her eyes. "I know. It just never seems like it's enough and I don't know what more I can do."

Without a thought, he grabbed her face and kissed her. That kiss contained everything he had held back. He no longer wanted to do the job he had been hired to do. He forced all of his regret, his fear, his hope into that moment. His heart raced and his stomach bounced but he held her close. When he pulled back, his eyes met with a look of confusion. "Oh, wow, I'm so sorry. I misread you."

A puff of steam escaped her lips. "No, it's fine. Don't worry," she responded quickly.

"No, it's not ok. I shouldn't have just presumed that you wanted that. I should've asked or something." He pulled away and stumbled over his words.

Haydeez turned towards the jeep. "We should really get those kids home. I'm sure someone is worried about them," she said. "We should let someone know that thing is dead too and where to find the other bodies."

"Right," Steve quickly answered. "It's best to let the authorities know it's over. We should go now."

Haydeez jumped into the jeep and started the ignition. Steve climbed in behind her. Neither said another word while they drove to the nearest town.

Chapter 18

After they dropped the children with the police, gave a believable story about why they were in the woods in the first place, and gave directions to where the bodies were, Haydeez and Steve headed back towards her home. Silence filled the jeep as neither was prepared to discuss what had happened.

They both jumped when her phone rang. Thankful for the break, she grabbed it and pushed the button a little too hard. "What happened, Linx?"

"The egg got away but so did I. Creepy snake lady tried to eat me. It was not pleasant to say the least," he said. "She did some spooky stuff with my mind too. I'll tell you about it when you get back. But, Pandora has the egg and I have my life. I don't really want to call it a total win but hey, I'm still here."

Haydeez slammed her hand on the door. "Damn! Ok, so we're going to need to find that egg before she does anything with it. Get home and we'll figure something out there. We're not too far off."

"How did it go?" Linx asked.

Haydeez cleared her throat. "No more Teumessian fox. Even managed to save a couple kids." She paused for a moment. "But not all of them."

"Oh, love, it's not your fault. Those two kids will remember what you did for them forever. Never let the bad outweigh the good," Linx answered. "Yes, you are correct. It's absolutely tragic, but you gave those children back their lives. They probably thought they were done."

With a sigh, she said, "Thanks, Linx. See you soon."

•   •   •

By the time Haydeez returned home, Linx already had a fire started and snacks on the table. He silently clicked away at his laptop as Haydeez warmed herself by the flames.

"Guess we were a little further away than I thought," she said.

Linx kept his eyes on the screen and said, "You drive slower when you're thinking. You tend to take longer when you've got something on your mind. Is everything alright, love?"

Haydeez looked at him with wide eyes and said, "No, everything's fine. Just too many kids dying. I guess it's getting further under my skin than I thought." She stuffed a slice of apple in her mouth and stood up. "Be right back." Before anyone could say anything she turned around and left the room.

Linx looked at Steve and asked, "Did something happen? She seems a bit off today."

Steve shook his head. "Nope, nothing happened. Killed a fox, rescued some kids, got in the jeep, and came back here."

Linx looked at Steve and looked to where Haydeez had been moments before and shook his head. He cleared his throat and went back to his laptop. The click of the keys was a little bit louder as he silently focused on the task at hand. Even though the words were never spoken, Linx still knew something had happened. With every ounce of self-control, his eyes remained on the screen. However, the screen became a complete blur of anger.

Steve looked around the room as he waited for Haydeez to return. His body indicated how uncomfortable he was as he wrung his hands and shuffled back and forth from one foot to the other. He checked his watch a few times, and then finally gathered up the courage to break the awkward silence. "Wonder what's taking so long," he mumbled.

"I wouldn't know, now would I," Linx answered with a bit too much acid in his voice. "I'm not her keeper."

With a look of surprise, Steve asked, "Where's the hostility coming from? I'm here to help. If you don't want my help, say so."

"Don't want your help, mate," Linx snapped back as he looked up from the screen to stare daggers at Steve. "We're fine without you."

Steve took a moment to collect himself and then responded, "Well, it would appear that it's not up to you, *mate*. I think we should leave this to someone with a bit more class. How about you let the adults talk and you go play with your toys?"

Linx stood up and faced Steve. "You think making fun of my accent hurts my feelings? Try again. I've stood by her side in more fights than you can count. I've backed her up and saved her life and kept her from doing anything stupid," he paused. "Like you. Don't think for a moment that I won't stand in your way." He began to walk slowly towards Steve. "I will block you at every turn. I'll make sure that you don't get close enough for anything to happen." Linx stood in Steve's face.

Steve chuckled. "What makes you think nothing has happened yet? You don't know me and you sure as hell don't know what I'm capable of, boy. She needs a man to step up and hold onto, not some nerdy little kid that hides behind his computer when things get bad. I suggest you back up and let a man make her happy."

Linx smiled. "You don't know me either, mate. It would be a mistake for you to push me too far. Disposing of a body isn't new to me."

Haydeez came back in the room with a notebook and a laptop and stopped in her tracks. "What's going on, guys? Is there a problem?" She walked over to the coffee table and placed her things on the edge.

Steve smiled at Haydeez. "Of course not. Just having a chat amongst friends." He stepped away from Linx and dropped himself into a nearby chair. With his hands placed behind his head, he leaned back and relaxed. "No problem at all."

Linx picked up his laptop and began to walk out of the room. He did not want to allow his emotions to spew out at that moment. There was not really anything to say. Sure, Steve was cocky and self-serving but he was right. Linx knew nothing about him. He also did not know what had happened between the two of them. Obviously, it was consensual because the guy is still here. Haydeez would never allow someone to hurt her again. Linx knew that. The only conclusion he could come to was that she liked Steve and whatever happened, Haydeez had wanted it.

Haydeez looked at Steve and then turned to Linx. "Hold on, what's going on?" she asked as she caught up with Linx on the staircase to the basement.

"Why don't you tell me," Linx whispered. "You come back here acting all strange and then you tell me 'nothing is wrong'. I don't buy it. Something happened and you're hiding it from me." He stopped at the bottom of the stairs. "Is something going on with him? Are you guys together now?"

Haydeez chuckled. She whispered, "Together? We hardly know each other. I'd say that the only thing we are doing is getting to know each other. I mean, yeah, I like working with him. It's not like I planned any of this. He's strong and protective," she paused for a moment.

Linx sighed. "Right." He turned back to the room and sat at one of the tables. "I'll be down here if you too want to do a little more getting to know each other although it would appear you already know enough." He yanked open his laptop and waited for the screen to load.

"Excuse me? Do you really think I'd just go out and screw someone I've only just met?" Haydeez asked incredulously. "I really thought you knew me better than that."

"Well, love, Steve seems to think there's more there. So, what would you have me believe? He acts like you've already done the deed and you tell me you haven't. You haven't exactly been completely honest with me lately, have you? Who would you have me believe?" he asked.

Haydeez scoffed. "Me! What's wrong with you? I would think a friend would want me to find someone that I enjoy being around instead of squelching any chance for happiness that might come my way."

With his eyes closed, Linx threw his head back and groaned. "Well at least I know where I stand now," he answered.

"What does that even mean? What the hell did I do to you? You know what? I'm going upstairs to try to solve this thing. If you want to help, fine. If not, I just don't care anymore. This is more important than his feelings or your feelings or even mine. Feelings don't matter right now. Lives matter and people are going to keep losing them if we don't step up our game." She turned and put her foot on the bottom step. With a hand on the rail, she paused. "Just so you know, it was a kiss, initiated by him after I killed the fox. That's it. So whatever your brain is cooking up, you might want to shut off the burner because it's overdone." She walked up the steps and left Linx in the basement alone.

Haydeez stood at the top of the steps and sighed. She paused with her hand on the door. So many thoughts passed through her mind. She opened the door and shoved it out of the way.

Steve sat on the couch. He jumped up as she came into the room. "Everything alright?" he asked.

"Just fine," she answered shortly. She moved past him without a glance in his direction. "Going out for a ride," she added.

"Need company?" he asked and took a step.

Haydeez pulled a coat from the closet in the foyer. "Nope," she answered and slammed the door.

Steve stood in the living room with his mouth open. He stared at the door with his brow furrowed.

A loud yell from the basement caused him to spin around. He ran to the door and opened it. "You alright down there?" he shouted.

"Mind your business, mate," Linx shouted up the stairs.

Steve quietly closed the door and walked back to the living room. He dropped down on the couch and mumbled, "Well, I guess I'll just stay here then."

•   •   •

Haydeez walked out the door and stood in front of her Jeep. Her eyes and fingertips followed the stitches on the worn but well-loved top. She felt the rough patches and traced each individual loop. She pulled out her keys and stopped.

The sound of the horses in the barn floated across the field. Haydeez turned to face the pasture.

In a matter of minutes, she had pulled a large Belgian draft horse from a stall and threw a heavy blanket over its back. She nimbly climbed the gate and hopped up onto the horse. Her small frame looked out of place on the massive creature but she did not care. She leaned her body against its neck and ran her fingers through the almost white mane. "I think we both need some fresh air, Jarl. What do you think?"

The horse stamped his hoof heavily and nickered.

"Sounds like a 'yes' to me," Haydeez said with a smile. She twisted her fingers into Jarl's mane and gripped tightly. She dug her heels hard into his ribs and yelled, "Ho!"

Jarl took off at a run. Clouds of snow kicked up behind him as he raced out onto her property. Steam escaped his nostrils like an old locomotive.

He pushed his legs harder and faster with every stride. His body thundered out to the open, white meadow.

Haydeez took a deep breath of the icy air. She shook her entire body. As she released the breath, a loud yell accompanied it. The yell turned into a laugh and she had to make a conscious effort to not fall off the horse.

Trees flew past in an evergreen haze. Haydeez pulled out her ponytail and unzipped her jacket. Her hair fluttered as she threw her head back. The crisp air kissed her face, chilled her skin, and tugged at her jacket. She squeezed her knees to hold her body in place and spread her arms out wide. With a sigh, she said, "This is why I'm here." She leaned forward, fell onto Jarl's neck, and wrapped her arms around it. Her hair mixed and mingled with the horse's mane as she breathed in his scent.

The raw earthy smell of the horse always grounded her. She did not need to speak, did not need a saddle or bridle. Jarl knew what she needed. He could feel her emotions. Sometimes she wanted to play, sometimes she wanted to look at the scenery and take a slow walk. Right now, all she wanted to do was run. So that is what he did.

They had been a match from the moment she saw him. Everyone told her she should probably look for a smaller horse, perhaps a pony, to suit her needs. They said that a woman her size would not be able to handle a stallion of this magnitude. All she said to them was "Give me my horse." She would have ridden him home from there if she did not have to take him across the ocean.

Haydeez closed her eyes and concentrated on Jarl's heartbeat. The crunch of the snow and the heavy hoof beats disappeared. Her finger tips pressed against the muscles in his neck as she pushed her cheek up against his fur and listened. The swift steady thump pulled her into a place where nothing can bother her. Pandora was gone. The creatures were gone. Her problems were gone.

"You're the only man that never aggravates me or makes me choose. You're my big, furry happy place," she said as she squeezed his neck. "Thank you," she whispered and buried her face into his mane.

He took her down a wide path between snow covered trees. They slowed to a trot and Haydeez lifted her head. She looked around and soaked up the scenery. The crisp snow glittered on everything. There were no tracks through the snow on the ground. No sounds filled the air. Nothing disturbed her this far into her property.

"What do you think, Jarl? Sometimes I feel helpless, like I don't know what I'm doing. I mean, I go out there and hunt. I'm good at what I do, but now," she paused for what felt like several minutes. "Now I have to figure out what Pandora is doing before she does it and stop her from destroying the world. I have to do all of this while keeping her weird creatures from eating children or stealing babies or whatever they're doing. Then, I have to deal with this guy that obviously has a thing for me and I'm not saying that I want to go totally down that road, but would it be so bad to walk a mile or two to see if it's worth the trip? It's crazy. I don't know what I'm doing right now but I'm expected to be calm and know exactly how to handle everything and make everyone happy in the process. Jarl, what am I supposed to do?" she asked.

Jarl shook his head and snorted.

"Makes perfect sense," she said.

He nodded his head as if to agree with her.

"Probably shouldn't leave the two of them back at the house alone for too long. They're not exactly best friends," she said to Jarl and rubbed his neck.

Without any other signal, the horse turned around easily and followed the hoof prints back to the stable.

Haydeez slid gracefully off Jarl's back. She brushed him and led him back to his stall. With her hands on the sides of his muzzle, Jarl leaned close to her and rubbed against her cheek. Her eyes closed. "Nchaynzeh," she whispered in Shoshoni. "Thank you again. You always ease my mind." She locked the stall and headed back into the house.

Linx came through the basement door as Haydeez opened the front door. "How's your boyfriend?" he asked jokingly.

She took off her coat and hung it up in the closet. "Perfect as always," she said calmly. "Hot chocolate? Sounds good," she added and walked to the kitchen. Her cheeks were red and hair was a mess. She ignored Steve who sat confused on the couch.

Linx followed her through the door. "Everything ok?" he asked tentatively.

She paused with a mug in her hand and thought for a moment. "Actually, I think it is. I just need to remind myself to take time away from everything. Besides, Jarl missed me a little." She smiled. "He likes our rides as much as I do."

Linx nodded. He took the mug from Haydeez and grabbed a second one. "He does get a bit antsy when you're gone for a while." He poured milk into a sauce pan and put it on a burner. With his eyes fixed on the pot, he added, "Jarl's not exactly a fan of me most days. Sometimes I think you tell him stuff to make him hate me so it's harder to take care of him while you're gone."

Haydeez laughed. "Why would I want to do that? I want him to be fed, not ignored. He decides who he likes on his own. I don't influence him." She chuckled as she pulled a green crazy straw from one of the drawers. "Look, I know everything is coming down on us all at once and now there's a new person in the mix. You know I don't just jump into things. I know how to take care of myself but," she paused and caught his eye. "I appreciate your concern. Ok?"

Linx sighed. "Fine. Sorry I worry," he smiled.

Chapter 19

Pandora stood over the phenix egg. She moved her hands in circles in the air. Her fingertips glowed as she made symbols above the egg. A low hum filled the air all around her.

The egg wobbled and pulsed. Tiny vibrations rippled out from it and flowed into the ground. They spread beyond Pandora's location as they called to the first man and woman. The egg sent out the call for them that it was time for them to be together.

Pandora forced the call before its time. She wanted to find the pair and stop them from dying together. This would ensure that mankind would not survive and her plans would be completed. She smiled and chanted in a long dead language.

The egg glittered with its own excitement as it found the first of the two.

"Come to the call. It will all be over soon, human," Pandora whispered.

The sky darkened and the air grew thick as if a great heat had settled in and had no plans of disbursing. The waters in the nearby lake began to boil and steam. Dead fish and frogs began to float to the surface and the smell of cooked fish filled the air.

Pandora breathed deeply and the orb in the middle of the dial glowed bright. Her body glistened with sweat and excitement. She reached out through the egg in search of the second half.

"Where are you? You cannot resist the call. You must come. Your other half will be here to die by your side," she mumbled. Her voice trembled with anticipation. The heat caused a steam so thick a person would not be able to see their hand if it was poking them in the eye, but Pandora ignored it.

She embraced it and used it to force back into the egg for the power it needed. The heat formed a circle to call the other half. It searched the earth, called to the woman. A spectral hand reached out and touched the mind of every female on the planet.

Finally, the invisible fingers brushed against the brain of the first woman. It tickled the spot in her mind that held the secret of who she really was, who she had been since the beginning of mankind. It flipped the switch and pulled her towards Pandora and the egg.

"Soon, you will both be here and you will die by my hand. I will revel in your death and the end of man on earth. My purpose will finally be fulfilled," she breathed heavily.

The first pair had been found. She could release the power. Her body slumped to the ground as the heat exploded around her. She heaved a sigh. "Too much power. I have not grown enough yet. I will need to force the Chimera out to gain her attention. She will need to destroy him so that I may gain his essence." Her body shuddered. "It will need to happen soon." She closed her eyes and allowed her body to sink slowly into the ground.

Chapter 20

Haydeez sat on the couch next to Steve. They looked at the laptop in confusion.

"I have no idea where to even look," Steve said. "This is all so confusing to me." He rubbed his eyes and stretched. "Explain to me again how we're going to find this egg?"

Haydeez leaned back on the couch. "We look for weather anomalies first because all these things seem to center around some weird weather thing. Then, if we can't find her that way, we look for other stuff like bizarre deaths, strange disturbances, things like that."

"So, we're just kind of shooting in the dark and hoping to hit a target. Good plan," Steve answered.

With a look of complete disgust, Haydeez said, "Shooting in the dark? Do you think this is my first time? Without some kind of signature, it's going to be very difficult to follow her. We have nothing from the egg, nothing from her. How else would you like to handle this investigation? By all means, if you think you can find her faster, feel free to try." She crossed her arms and pulled her feet up onto the couch. "Go right ahead."

Steve chuckled. "Fine. You're in charge. We'll do it your way." He picked up the laptop and began to search for the weather anomalies.

Haydeez smiled. "My way, exactly." She looked over his shoulder at the screen.

Steve inhaled her scent. "So, are we ever going to talk about it or just pretend like it didn't happen," he said. His eyes remained on the screen.

Haydeez groaned. "I hate talking about feelings and stuff. Can't we just forget it and find the egg? That's what I'm good at."

"I see we're opting for pretend then," Steve answered. "It's just that," he paused. "I didn't mean to make you uncomfortable or anything. I just thought it felt right and I went for it. I'm sorry if it screwed things up. I would take it back if that was an option." He smirked.

"Can't take back a kiss. Once it happens, you're pretty much stuck with the consequences," Haydeez said.

Steve smiled again. "What do I do if I like the consequences? Should I do it again?"

"Do what again?" Linx asked, a look of irritation on his face. He looked back and forth between Haydeez and Steve, and then rolled his eyes. "Nevermind. Forget I asked. I've been analyzing weather patterns to see if I could figure out a path or something, anything that might lead us to Pandora." He sighed. "I noticed something that I thought you might be interested in. For this time of year, everything in the northern hemisphere tends to get colder. But check this out." He spun the laptop around and pointed. "Right there. Do you see the spike? Seems a bit warm don't you think."

Haydeez stared at the screen for a moment and shrugged. "Looks like we have a place to start. Keep an eye out for anything else like this. We'll go check it out. Maybe she left something."

Linx sighed. "Sure, I'll stay here and look for anything else out of the ordinary." He turned and walked away. "I'll call if I find anything," he added half-heartedly over his shoulder.

"We still don't know what she was doing there," Haydeez mumbled to herself. Then, her eyes opened wide. She sighed heavily. "That's it. She's activated the egg early. She's trying to bring the first couple to her. If she kills them and they aren't together, who knows what could happen. We need to stop her. We have to get that egg."

Steve looked on in awe. "I truly hope you're right. I mean, I hope we can stop her. I'm not ready to be wiped from existence." He stood up. "We should get going right?" he asked.

Haydeez picked up the laptop and walked away. "Give me a minute."

•　•　•

Linx heard Haydeez come down the stairs but kept his eyes on the laptop.

"What's going on with you today?" she asked before her feet touched the last step. "If you've got something to say then just say it."

Linx closed his eyes and sighed. "It just seems unlike you to let someone you hardly know into your home, let alone down here. I get that I didn't find anything on him but are you sure you should be traveling alone with him? There's something I don't trust about him, love. He was on his own hunt but he's just forgotten it and stuck around to help you? Who does that?" He scratched his head. "I've never known you to be so trusting of someone you just met. I just don't get it."

Haydeez shuffled her feet and closed her eyes for a moment. "I don't know. I just feel like he's supposed to be here for some reason. There's something about him that I trust. Look, you of all people know I can take care of myself." She looked at Linx who had yet to make eye contact with her. "Ok, so he's attractive and, as much as I try to deny it, I like being around him. It's nice to have someone attracted to me without wanting something in return or being nice while hiding their true intentions. Just trust me. I'll be fine."

Linx scoffed. "Without wanting something in return... Right. Fine. Just call if you need anything. And please, be careful, love," Linx answered. He caught her gaze and held it for what seemed like hours. "I can't do this without you."

Haydeez smiled. "I know. You're pretty helpless without me." She turned, put her foot on the bottom step, and then paused. "I'll be safe. I promise," she added and made her way back up the stairs.

•   •   •

Haydeez and Steve drove into the heart of the location Linx provided. The ground should have been covered in fresh snow but was instead covered in dead wet grass. Haydeez stopped the jeep and looked around. "Now that looks weird. Even if she melted the snow, it's snowed since then. We shouldn't be able to see the grass." She left the jeep and pulled out her phone to take some pictures. "I'm sending some images, Linx. Check this out."

Steve opened the door. "Is it just me or is it a little warm here?" he asked.

"Well, it's certainly not you," Haydeez said with a smirk.

"Mind scanning the area for me, love? She may have left some of her residual energy floating around. Would love to snag some," Linx said into her earpiece. "If I didn't know better, I would say that she just left, but it's been several hours. That must have been some spell she cast."

Haydeez scanned the area with a small hand-held device. "I can feel the energy here. There shouldn't be a problem getting something for us to use. If she called the first couple together, we need to get to her soon. We don't know what will happen if she kills them." The device beeped and Haydeez smiled. "Got it. Let's get out of here," she said to Steve.

He nodded. "So, that's it. Nothing else to do here then? I guess I thought there was going to be..." he paused and looked around. "More."

"Not all the time. This scanner can't search. I need to get the readings into the computer at home so we can start looking for her," she answered. "The computer has a better range." She hopped into the jeep. "You coming or would you rather just stand out here in the middle of nowhere for a bit?"

The engine roared back to life. Haydeez pulled out of the field and made her way back to the road. Snow crunched under her tires. "We're headed back now, Linx. Anything else we should know about?"

After a moment of silence on the other end, Linx answered. "Nope, haven't seen anything else yet. It's oddly quiet right now. In fact, I'm a little concerned at how quiet it actually is." He paused again. "There's usually something, a storm, weird creature sightings, anything that says she's around but there's just nothing."

"How can there be nothing?" Haydeez asked. "She has to be somewhere."

With a sigh, Linx answered, "Well, wherever she is, she's quiet. She's probably waiting for the couple to get to her."

Haydeez stared at the road, lost in thought. After several long, silent minutes, she said, "See if you can get any more information about the egg. Find out if it has to be in a specific place for the rebirth to work. Even if it just tells the type of area, at least it's somewhere to start."

"I'll contact Piven, see what he's got," Linx answered.

Chapter 21

A crash boomed from behind a closed door followed by a roar. Miko stood with his hand poised to knock. When the roar ended, he waited a few moments and then knocked.

"What?" the voice boomed behind the door.

"You have a guest, Mr. Campanos. Your young benefactor has dropped by for a visit, sir," Miko answered.

Stavros growled. "Come in."

Miko opened the door and ushered Pandora into the dark room.

With a smile, she said, "Thank you, Mr. Miko." She walked into the dark as if the room was clearly lit. Pieces of broken furniture littered the floor. She avoided them with ease and found her way to one of the only places to sit.

"Good evening, Mr. Stavros. I see you're not doing well. I'm so sorry about that. Is there anything I can help you with, Mr. Stavros?" Pandora asked innocently.

Stavros clawed at a pile of broken furniture. "You can remove these voices from my head so I can think clearly again," he growled. "Every time I try to decide what to do, my every thought is disrupted by someone who has no idea how to run this family."

His wife hissed. "Perhaps it's because we're tired of hearing about how you want to kill people. Maybe we'd like to think of other things as well."

Stavros reached back and grabbed the serpent head with a massive clawed hand. "Watch your tongue, woman! You know where your place is!" He yelled.

Pandora watched as her creature attempted to destroy itself. She sighed. "You must learn to work together or I may have to take back this wonderful gift. The Chimera is three parts of a whole. It is a delicate balance of those three parts that makes it such a formidable force. Perhaps I have not chosen correctly. Perhaps another would be able to handle the strength of this gift."

Stavros snapped his head in Pandora's direction and growled. He leapt over the pile and towered over her tiny body. He roared into her young face. Warm spittle flew from his sharp white teeth. "How dare you think to challenge me?" he bellowed.

The child sat up straight as saliva flew past her pristine skin. "Your anger will be your end," she said quietly. She sat patiently until he was done with his tirade, then she spoke to him again. "You act as if you have allowed your child to take over. The Chimera does not throw petty tantrums. The Chimera utilizes all of its parts as one. It works as an army all on its own to take on its enemies. It spreads fear on sight and cripples foes with the sound of its massive roar." She looked around the room. "It doesn't plan or strategize. It strikes hard and fast. Do you understand, Mr. Stavros?"

A low rumble vibrated in his chest. "How am I to attack when I can barely leave this room?"

Pandora smiled. "I will give you," she paused. "A guide, someone to assist you with any of your troubles and help you to work together as one unit. I will return in a moment with someone." She popped up from the chair before he could respond and bopped out of the room.

She passed Miko in the hall and headed upstairs. With a giggle, she looked around the room. "Hello. I have a question. Mr. Stavros needs someone to assist him. It's a terribly important job. Is there anyone who would like to help him?"

The people looked around at each other. A man stood up and said, "I can help."

Pandora shook her head. "No, you won't do." Her gaze moved around the room and fell upon a woman. With a smile, she began to walk towards the woman. "I believe you will do nicely. Mr. Stavros could use your assistance. He would be most grateful if you accept his request. Would you help him?" She held out her hand for the woman to take it.

A look of confusion crossed her face and she glanced at the people around her. "What do I need to do?" she asked.

"Just come with me," Pandora answered.

The woman took Pandora's hand and followed her down the stairs. They walked past Miko and back into the room. Pandora closed the door behind them and the room was completely black.

"Mr. Stavros? Are you here?" the woman asked tentatively. "You needed my help?"

Pandora held onto the woman and asked, "Are you willing to help tonight?"

"Yes, of course," she answered.

Pandora whispered a few words and a soft golden glow pulsed around her. The light grew and began to illuminate the rest of the room. A soft sound followed the glow. It sounded as if a gentle breeze brushed against crystal pieces in a wind chime. A song flowed out of the golden glow and formed a silvery cloud in front of the woman.

"What is that?" she asked with a quiver in her voice. Her eyes grew wide as her body froze in place. She was mesmerized by the spectacle.

"This is how you will help. You will be his guide. You will help him control his beast and conquer his enemies," Pandora said. The glow grew stronger and bathed the room in a beautiful, soft light. The Chimera was visible as it stood over a pile of rubble. The snake's head swayed back and forth patiently behind his massive head.

The woman gasped. Her mouth froze open before a question could be asked. Fear kept her glued to the same spot. She no longer noticed the silver figure in front of her as it took stock.

"She has accepted, sirenum. She is willing to help," Pandora said sweetly. "You may take her."

The mist swayed back and forth for a moment in an attempt to catch the woman's gaze. Finally, they locked eyes. Soft chimes pranced playfully throughout the room. The woman's body grew limp and began to sway along with the mist. The silvery fog moved closer and closer until it melted into the woman's body. She let out a gasp in ecstasy.

Pandora watched as the woman's body glistened and sparkled. She moaned and writhed on the floor while everything transformed. Her transformation was more pleasurable than the others had been. The song from the creature had left the woman in a state of joy instead of fear. Every inch of her body sparkled. She wore a silken gown that barely covered anything. Her toes curled and she stretched across the carpet.

Her eyes fluttered open and she smiled, "Aunt Pandora, such a pleasant surprise. Much gratitude for releasing me from that wretched prison." She rolled gracefully onto her stomach and purred. "What services might I provide this evening?" She looked around the room and stopped on the Chimera. "Greetings, brother. You appear to be troubled. Is there something that ails you?" She rolled over, popped up to her feet, and walked toward him.

"You will be his guide, my niece. He is unsure in this new world and could use your particular skills," Pandora said. "You will watch over him and, should the need arise, you will help to calm him."

The siren bowed. "At your request, Aunt Pandora." She reached out to touch him. As she spoke, it sounded like rain drops that danced across a lake. "I will keep you safe, brother." She moved her fingers through his fur and purred. "You are an incredible specimen. Everyone will fall before you or die beneath your feet."

A low rumble began deep in the Chimera's belly as he rubbed his face against her delicate fingers. He closed his eyes and leaned into her touch. The serpent head slid around and flicked its tongue to taste the siren's skin. It wrapped gently around her leg and slid up her hip. The snake flicked its tongue against her other hand and sat peacefully while she spoke to the lion's head.

"You have no equal, brother. Even one such as myself could fall before you. Do you wish for me to serve you, to ensure your triumph?" she asked. Her words rolled off her tongue seductively. With every word, the chimera visibly calmed until he was finally just a lump of fur and scales on the floor.

Pandora smiled. "You've done well. I will need you to stay by him and make sure he stays focused on the larger future and not just his pathetic human desires," she said. "I still need him."

The siren bowed. "Of course, Aunt Pandora. "He will remain a soldier in your war, I assure you."

Chapter 22

Linx heard the sound of footsteps on the stairs behind him. He turned to the laptop and said, "Hold that thought just a moment please. Thank you." As he turned back around, Haydeez appeared in the doorway and, with a smile, he said, "I think we may have something." He gestured to the laptop. "Mr. Piven has done a bit of digging and has found notes on the egg that may be of help to us." He looked back at the screen and said, "Whenever you're ready."

"Thank you, son. Haydeez, it's such a pleasure to speak to you again. I would ask if things are going well but your friend has already filled me in on that." He shook his head. "It's such a shame that she got away but don't fret. I've found a passage that refers to the resurrection." He pulled a large worn book onto his lap and looked at the pages. "When the egg activates, the first man and first woman will converge without knowledge or understanding of their purpose. The egg will call to them from anywhere on the earth and they will meet on their place of birth. Once there, they will gain the knowledge of who they are and begin the process of passing." He paused for a moment. "The place of their birth. They're reborn anywhere in the world but they were only 'born' once. If this is the first man and woman, we need to figure out which one they're referring to because each mythology has its own idea of who was created first. If we go by the Greeks, Pandora was the first woman. If it's Adam and Eve, they're from the deserts in the Middle East. In Norse, it would be Ask and Emlba and we'd be looking in Scandinavia."

"So, we're back to square one," Linx sighed. "Any idea which one we're looking for?" he asked Cornelius.

He looked in the book and scanned the pages. After several minutes passed in silence, he looked back at the screen. "Considering that the phenix egg comes from Greek mythology, I would assume Pandora, but she wouldn't need to call herself. I'm sorry, dear. I'm at a loss."

Haydeez sat down for a moment and rubbed her forehead. She had no idea where to go from here. Her body had already started to shut down for sleep.

Linx looked over and sighed. The expression on his face showed that he knew exactly what she needed. He stood up, walked over to her and said, "Time for bed, love. Sleep on it, let it sink in, and we'll start fresh tomorrow." He helped her up and guided her to the stairs. As she started to walk up, he turned back to the laptop and said, "Thank you, sir. We'll be in touch."

Cornelius nodded. "I'll contact you if I find anything else. Take care, dear," he said as he ended the video.

Steve stood alone in the room. He dropped his arms to his sides and shrugged. After he looked around the empty basement for a moment, he then called up the stairs. "Guess I'll just show myself out," he yelled.

"Yup," Linx called back to him.

Steve shook his head and chuckled to himself as he climbed up the stairs.

• • •

In the darkness of Haydeez's bedroom, the soft tick tock of the clock on the wall tapped the seconds away. She slept peacefully as her chest rose and fell with each breath. Her body nestled comfortably into the warm plush blankets.

Her body tensed and she gasped as her eyes flew open. She bolted up. "They're not born!" she shouted. "They're created! We had it all wrong!" She breathed heavily as her eyes adjusted to the darkness. "Linx, we had it wrong!"

The covers flew into the air. Haydeez jumped out of bed and threw on a robe. She flung open her door and ran down the hall. "Linx! Get up! I think I figured it out!" She pounded on his door.

Linx jumped out of bed and ran to his bedroom door. "What happened, love? Are you alright?"

With a grin, Haydeez answered, "I think I've got it. Come with me. Hurry." She spun around and ran down the stairs.

Linx stood in the doorway, eyes red, and rubbed the sleep away. "Am I really surprised?" he asked himself and followed her.

.   .   .

Linx nodded. "That actually makes more sense than anything else we've come up with so far. It definitely narrows things down for us. Any idea who you think it is?" he asked.

Haydeez turned the screen. "Ok, so I've picked the ones that sounded like they fit what we're looking for and this is what I have."

Linx scanned the list with a confused look on his face. "Why not Adam and Eve?" Linx asked.

Haydeez smiled proudly. "Good question. Adam and Eve had Cain and Abel, both male. No mention of ever having a daughter. So, while Adam and Eve were the first man and woman 'created' by the Christian God, they were not born. They don't count. What we're looking for is the first man and woman 'born', so we need to know who the first children were."

Linx sat back and stared at the list. There weren't many names on there. "Should we call Piven? I'm sure he'd like to know. Maybe get his input," Linx said.

"Yup, sure," Haydeez said as she scanned the list.

Linx shook his head and chuckled. He dialed the number and looked at the clock. "You do know what time it is, love?"

"Nope, no idea," she mumbled. "What time is it?"

He quickly hung up the phone. "It's 4 am. He's probably asleep. I mean, I know he said to call if we found anything, but he probably assumed that we'd get sleep and call in the morning," he said as the phone rang. "Or he'll be up and call us back. I've been wrong before, not the first time. Hello? We did. She found something and we wanted to run it by you. Hold on." He clicked a button. "Ok, go ahead, love."

"Hey, sorry to wake you but I think I figured it out," she said.

Cornelius cleared his throat and asked, "So what are we dealing with, dear?"

Haydeez smiled. "Glad you're on the team. So, I was thinking about it and it says they go back to where they were born. Well, in mythology, the first man and woman were created, not born. So, all these first couples would be off the list. What we need to be looking at are the first children of the first couples. I've already taken Adam and Eve off the list because they had two boys and there's never mention of a daughter."

"Clever girl," Cornelius mumbled. "Well, in that case, what have you got so far?"

Haydeez grabbed a piece of paper and said, "Ok, I've been looking through and there's just so many first couples that follow the same lines, both males. It's like the newer mythologies looked to the older ones, copied what they liked, and changed it to suit their needs. So, that eliminates a big chunk. What we have left is very little. However," she paused. "Right now I'm looking at Japanese and Greek. The Japanese doesn't specify a man and woman. It only says male and female children. So, I'd say that one's out. The Greek, however, took a little digging but I've got some ancient references to Pandora's daughter, Pyrrha, and her son, Graecus. Now, most places say that the son was actually her great grandson."

"So why are we considering him then?" Linx asked.

"Because I found the text that references him. The translation is wrong. According to the translations, Zeus laid with Pandora II, who was supposedly Pandora's granddaughter, but, when you read it correctly, it says he laid with Pandora twice. Everyone knows how much Zeus loved coming down to the humans in one form or another and having his pick of sexual partners. In this instance, Pandora gave birth to a son, the first man born of this earth," she smiled as excitement spilled from her eyes.

Linx just stared at her for a moment. "Wow."

"Well, this puts a little kink in things. You're looking for Pandora's children?" Cornelius asked.

Several moments passed as the three sat in silence and contemplated all the problems that would arise. Then Haydeez cleared her throat and spoke. "Wait a minute. If she destroys man, she'll be destroying her own children. Could anyone really be that horrible? I mean, I know the saying 'you always hurt the ones you love' but isn't this taking that a little too far?"

"I don't believe she really cares, dear. You need to look at this like she's just another psychopath and not a mother. Don't humanize her. She'll become the victim and you'll lose your nerve. No matter what, she needs to be stopped. She can't be allowed to kill her children," Cornelius said. "I know it's hard to believe that someone would want to do this but just remember: she was created to destroy, nothing more."

Haydeez sighed. "It's just so weird."

"Just look at it as protecting innocents," Linx chimed in. "Her children are innocent. They didn't ask to be in this cycle for all eternity. They need to be saved and that's your job. Forget the details."

"Sometimes the details aren't that easily dismissed but I get what you're saying," she answered. "So, at some point we're headed to Greece I suppose. But how long do we have before they get together?" she asked.

Cornelius cleared his throat. "It takes time for them to make their trip. You've got," he paused. The only sound was the flip of pages through the receiver. "Ah, you've got a few months before they come together. Hopefully that gives you enough time to get to their initial birth place and prevent the end of the human race," he said matter-of-factly. "Considering everything was centered around specific areas in ancient Greece, it shouldn't be too hard to narrow down the correct location."

Haydeez smiled at Linx. "Are you offering to research for me, Piven?"

With a chuckle, he said, "My dear, research is what I do. Give me some time. I'll see what I can find for you. Besides, you need to focus on that gorgon she released. Euryale is utterly hateful and will need to be destroyed."

She nodded in agreement. "So true. We'll get her taken care of and you find me that location." She paused for a moment. "You know, I wanted to meet you for some time now but I never thought I'd be working with you." She chuckled. "I appreciate the help."

"Of course, dear. This is more action than I get to see in a year," Cornelius laughed. "I'll be in touch." The phone clicked.

Linx shook his head and rubbed his eyes. "Well, that was productive. What do you say we go back to sleep? Sounds like we've got a little time before the world ends." He yawned.

Haydeez nodded. "One thing checked off the to-do list. I have no idea how many left." She turned and walked up the stairs.

Steve quickly tapped his fingers as he waited for Miko to answer. "Finally. Is this job over yet? Does Mr. Campanos still need me?" he asked quickly.

Miko cleared his throat. "Is everything alright, Mr. Osbourne? You sound a bit breathless and disoriented. Are you not up to this task that you have been paid for?"

With a huff, Steve answered. "Do you even know what's going on? Things are getting really weird and I don't think I can keep her busy for much longer. She's not normal, Miko!" He began to pace. "What are you not telling me, Miko? What am I in the middle of?" he asked frantically.

"Mr. Osbourne, you have been paid to keep the young woman busy. Ms. Blackhawk is to be kept out of the way, safe, but out of the way. It would appear that you're not capable of handling yourself any longer," Miko answered calmly. "I will be happy to discuss your current situation with Mr. Campanos and terminate your employ with us. We will be happy to find a new associate to take your place. Rest assured we will no longer bring you into our endeavors as you are not capable of handling more stressful situations." He paused.

"Stressful? Miko, do you even know what I've been dealing with out here? No amount of money could cover any of this!" Steve shouted. "I shot at a crazy snake lady! I emptied my gun. Not a single scratch on her! Then, this Haydeez lady throws the crazy snake lady out the window! She threw her out the window, Miko! Are you hearing me? Then, if that wasn't enough, we hunted a giant fox. This thing was bigger than a lion and it ate little kids, man! I've killed a lot but this thing left more dead bodies than I could count. And she ran *towards* it! This is not the job I thought it was going to be. I'm flying blind here and quickly losing control. You need to tell me the whole story, Miko."

Miko cleared his throat again. "Did you just give me an order, Mr. Osbourne? You know how we deal with orders, Mr. Osbourne. Perhaps you would be interested in retracting your previous statement before something bad were to happen to you."

"Retract my statement? Miko, this isn't normal! What the hell is going on?" he yelled. "I'm not dealing with ordinary people here and quite frankly

I've been questioning some things since I signed on to this job." He paused and took a breath. "I didn't want to say anything at the time because Mr. Campanos pays very well but something seemed a bit off with him the night he called me in. After I saw his office, I thought a wild animal had trashed the place but that's not possible, right Miko? There are no wild animals in Boston, right Miko? Rats? Sure. Stray dogs? Of course. But something big enough to tear through a solid wooden desk? Of course not. Not in Boston. Or am I on the right track, Miko? Tell me what's happening because I feel like I've stepped into a weird world and I don't like being surprised like this."

"You were hired to keep the girl busy, Mr. Osbourne. That's all you need to know," Miko calmly replied. "What Mr. Campanos does is his own business."

Steve shouted. "No! That's not good enough. Does he have something in his office? Is there a wild animal in there?" Steve paused. "God, Miko. Mr. Campanos *is* a wild animal. What the hell is he, Miko? Was that him? Did he do that to his desk? I knew something was off. I heard growling. There wasn't something in his office. It was him! He tore apart the desk! The gashes, the noises, it was all him!" Steve shook his head to try to clear it but the images remained. "What is he, Miko?"

Miko raised his voice. "Mr. Campanos hired you for one reason. You do not need to ask questions that do not pertain to your job. This is not important for you to know. His business is his own."

"What is he, Miko?" Steve yelled. "What is he?"

"He's lost!" Miko yelled. "That's what he is! He is lost. He made a deal and lost himself. I've never seen him act this way. I don't know what happened. I see it every day and I still don't understand it. That little girl turned him into something unnatural. Magic isn't supposed to be real but I know what I saw. It was bad enough that he changed himself, but then he brought his family into it. His wife, his son, they're part of this thing too."

Steve sighed. "What is he, Miko?" he asked again.

"The Chimera. He's some kind of man, lion, snake, goat thing. The little girl called it Chimera. She told him it would help him achieve his goal of destroying the other mob bosses but not before she gets what she wants from him. I don't know what she is or what she wants but I know she's more dangerous than I am."

Steve chuckled. "You're kidding, right? A Chimera. Like from the Greeks and stuff? How could she make him into that? You've got to be seeing things."

Miko slammed his fist against the table. "I know what I saw. She said some weird stuff, and this cloud of smoke floated over to Mr. Campanos and his family. They all screamed and I watched while they came together into this thing. Look, I don't know what she wants with him but I know there's no going back now. He's lost himself completely."

"I have to tell her," Steve said. "She has to stop him." He hung up the phone before Miko had the chance to respond.

Chapter 23

The gate box buzzed. "Hello?" Linx said. They were not expecting anyone and uninvited guests are usually not welcome.

"It's Steve. I need to talk to Haydeez."

Linx dropped his head and groaned. "Yeah, just a minute," he answered. "Steve's here, Haydeez," he yelled over his shoulder. He pressed the button and waited by the door. When Steve knocked, Linx opened the door, crossed his arms, and said "What? Why are you here?"

"I don't have time for this. I need to talk to Haydeez," Steve said. "It's important."

Haydeez came down the stairs. "What's going on?" she asked. Her brow furrowed. "Is something wrong? You look upset."

"We need to talk," Steve answered, his voice breathy. "You need to know the truth."

As the apprehension rose, Haydeez motioned Steve into the house. "What do you mean by 'the truth'?" she asked. She motioned them all into the living room.

Steve took a deep breath. "Ok, first of all, just realize that it took a lot for me to come here and tell you all this. I could've kept it a secret but I wanted to be honest with you." He sat on the edge of the couch and took another deep breath.

"Ok, so what's the truth?" Haydeez asked warily.

As he let out the breath, Steve started. "This snake lady isn't the only thing out there. That egg you're looking for isn't the only problem you have. There's something in Boston you need to see. A mob boss by the name of Stavros Campanos made a deal with a little girl to turn himself into a Chimera. I don't know who the little girl is or where to find her or why she did it but I know he's more dangerous now than he ever was.

Apparently, this little girl is dangerous too but I don't really know anything about her." He sighed. "All I know is that Stavros is not himself. He transformed not only himself, but his family as well, into this thing. According to my source, they share a body in this creepy man, lion, snake, goat thing."

Haydeez looked at Linx. "Pandora. But why would she release the Chimera when Euryale already got her the egg? It doesn't make sense."

Linx shook his head. "You're right it doesn't make sense. Wait. How did you find out about this? You said you had a source. Who?"

Steve looked down at his hands for a moment.

Haydeez moved to put her hand on his arm. "How did you find out about all this?"

Steve closed his eyes. "His right hand man told me."

Linx narrowed his gaze. "Why would he do that, mate?"

"Because I pressed him. Because Mr. Campanos hired me to keep you busy," he answered. "The girl made a deal with him to give him a way to get what he wanted as long as he figured out a way to keep you busy while she did whatever it was that she needed to do. So he hired me. It was my job to distract you and keep your mind clouded while she was busy doing something else. That's why I asked you to coffee, asked you to the party, all of it."

Haydeez pulled her hand back as if she had touched a hot stove. "All of it?" she asked.

Steve looked up quickly, his eyes wide. "Wait. Not all of it. Not that. Just the stuff in the beginning when we met."

Haydeez stood up and stepped away from him. "Of course. Only the stuff that doesn't make you look a complete waste of flesh. Is that everything or is there more? What else has been a lie? What else were you paid to do?" she asked as her voice caught in her throat.

"No, wait, I swear that wasn't a lie." He stood up quickly. "I mean, I was hired to keep you busy and everyone has to meet somehow, right? Wow, that sounded terrible. I mean, no matter what, I'm still glad we met, no matter what the circumstances are. To be honest, I have no idea what's going on right now. I don't even know what a Chimera is or what that snake thing was. I'm just a bounty hunter. I catch criminals and bring them in when they jump bail. This is all new to me."

Haydeez shook her head. "So you're not a hunter? How did you know where to find me? How did Linx get a clear background on you?"

"Because I don't have a record. My background shows that I'm a bounty hunter. He wouldn't have found anything. Nothing links me to any of the, shall we say, unsavory population. I'm clean, on paper." He ran his hand through his hair. "Mr. Campanos told me how to find you because that girl told him where the woman was who had killed those kids. It was pretty easy. Look, I didn't know any of this was going on. I don't even know what to say. I don't know how to deal with all this. My boss is a weird creature. I was almost killed by a crazy snake lady. I rescued some kids from a giant killer fox. This is stuff from movies, not real life."

Haydeez took another step back. "This is real life for me. I do this every day. I see these things all the time and save lives. People like you don't actually know what's out there. You don't know how close danger is to you every day. I stopped a Loup Garou from killing an ancient Celtic god just a few months ago. I've taken out vamps, shapeshifters, and plenty of things that you couldn't even imagine. Why? Because someone has to and most people run screaming when faced with their worst nightmares." She planted her feet. "I grew up in this world. I tried to be normal like you. I tried to leave it, to be happy, married, start a family. It's hard to fake when you've seen someone eaten by a creature whose name you can't even pronounce. Normal problems seem petty after all this. Fighting over who forgot to pick up milk or if the bills were paid this month. I do what I do so people like you can have those fights. You don't belong here, Steve." She turned and began to walk away. "Thanks for the info. Linx can show you out." She walked towards the basement.

"Wait, please. I'm so sorry. I didn't want to hurt you," he called to her. As he took a step forward, Linx put a hand on his chest.

"Don't, mate. Just turn around and go. Forget this address. Forget us. Forget her. You don't belong in this world," Linx whispered, eyes full of hatred.

Steve looked between Linx and the door that Haydeez had just closed. He sighed. "Fine. I'll go but you know that I can't forget her." He turned and walked to the front door. "I know my way out."

• • •

A crash sounded from the basement followed by a scream. Linx stood at the door and waited for a moment. He knocked and cracked the door slightly. "Is it safe for me to come down, love?"

Haydeez groaned. "Yeah, I'm not mad at you."

He walked down the steps and surveyed the mess. "Did that chair lie to you too?" he asked with a smile. "Do you need anything?"

Her shoulders slumped. "What the hell? I know he was annoying at first, and cocky. I really should learn to trust my initial instincts and not let my guard down. I thought he might be different." She rolled her eyes and groaned. "I sound like such a cliché. 'Maybe I can change him'," she said as she batted her eyelashes. "And of course he was a jerk, just like everyone else." She flopped onto the couch and closed her eyes.

"Not *everyone* else, but that's ok," Linx mumbled. "True, he was a complete waste but at least you know who you can trust." He sat down next to her and bumped her with his shoulder. "I know *I've* never lied to you, right?" He smiled.

She chuckled and shook her head. "No, not that I know of yet. But then again, I'm not really that great of a judge of character. So, who knows?"

He put his arm around her and squeezed. "You'll be fine. You took a chance. It didn't go anywhere. That's more than I've done, love. My life is here. How often do you see me go out and meet people?" He chuckled. "I wouldn't even know how to introduce myself. 'Hi, I'm Linx. I help my good friend, Haydeez, hunt weird creatures you didn't even know existed. Want to grab some coffee and talk about it?' I'd sound completely mental."

Haydeez chuckled. "You really don't do well in social situations." She sighed heavily. "So what do we do now?" She rested her head on his shoulder. "Every step we take forward ends with us crashing into a brick wall. I feel like we won't make it. She's already activated the egg. We've got Euryale out there doing," she paused. "I have no idea what she's doing out there but it can't be good. Now we have a Chimera out there too? Creatures I can handle but what is Pandora doing? I just have more questions than answers."

Linx stood up and stretched. "Then we find answers, love." He held out his hand. "It's what we do. Besides, who else is going to protect everyone?"

She took his hand and stood up. "You are my rock, Linx. So, which one do we find first?"

•　　•　　•

"So, an actual god killed the Chimera the first time. Great. So that means we're screwed." Linx threw up his arms and began to pace. "What is her problem?"

Haydeez laughed. "After all this research, you forgot everything you knew about Pandora? She was *created* for this. It's her purpose in life, her *only* purpose. Unfortunately for us, she's taking it very literally." She put her chin in her hand and sighed. "If she's trying to destroy man, why would she release the Chimera?" she mumbled to herself. "Why does she need that thing?"

Linx sat in front of the laptop and clicked away at the keyboard. "Did you know that there are major disasters right before a Chimera attack? I mean, we're talking Pompeii-style disasters. It's like an omen. Although, once it happens, the Chimera attack seems like overkill. Not to mention, who is actually going to be alive to see what the Chimera does? Wait, so how does anyone even know what it does?" he paused for a moment. Then, his eyes widened. "What if the disaster *is* the Chimera attacking?" He turned to Haydeez. "What if the Chimera is the one making the earthquake or the volcano erupt or whatever it is? This thing could take out cities or even a small country if it wanted to and nobody would even know."

"I guess that tells us who we need to look for first. Steve said that he was in Boston. It shouldn't be too hard to locate him. We just need to figure out how to stop him. It's not like either of us is a god or anything," she said. "According to the legend, Bellerophon shot the Chimera from above while riding on Pegasus. Well, that's simple enough." She dropped her head down and smacked it against the table with a loud thump. "It just gets better and better."

"There has to be another way," Linx said.

• • •

Steve listened to the ring of the cell phone as he waited for Miko to answer.

"Yes?" Miko said on the other end.

"Look, you said he's lost himself and there's no way he's coming back, right?" Steve asked. "So, how do we stop him then?"

Miko chuckled. "You really think it's that easy?"

"Don't play games with me, Miko. You're his right hand. You have to know something," Steve growled. "I'm not scared of you or what you're going to do to me. I don't care. You don't seem to realize what he's allied himself with and what's going to happen. That little girl is going to kill everyone, including Mr. Campanos and you. She's using him to get what she wants. It doesn't matter if he helped her or not. Apparently, she wants to kill everyone just because and when I say everyone I mean everyone on Earth, not just Boston. Do you get me, Miko? She needs to be stopped."

Miko sighed. "Are you sure you're not just overreacting to something? It seems to me that you might be a little inebriated, Mr. Osbourne. Perhaps you should consider stepping away from whatever poison you've taken a liking to today. It's inhibited your ability to think clearly."

"Miko!" Steve yelled. "I'm not drunk. I'm not high. I'm serious. After seeing what she did, you're still going to question what I'm telling you. That little girl is Pandora. She's trying to fulfill her purpose. She's going to kill everyone. Don't you get it? Why am I the only one freaked out over this? Doesn't anyone see the severity of this?" he screamed.

There was silence on the other end as Miko processed everything. After several minutes of nothing, Steve said, "Are you still there, Miko?"

He cleared his throat and answered, "I knew something was off about that girl. She should not have been that comfortable around Mr. Campanos. Someone like that making demands of him... I knew it wasn't right. I should've stopped him." He sighed heavily. "And now he's gone. His family is gone. I don't know what to do. A regular person? I know how to deal with that. Point and shoot, choke them into submission, but something that isn't really supposed to be alive? How do you beat that? I don't scare and if you speak about this to anyone else, you'll see exactly what I'm capable of but this is not natural. We shouldn't even be talking about this. I don't know any of that history stuff. The only thing I know about that Pandora girl is that she opened a box. I don't even know where to start."

Steve tapped his hand on the dashboard. "I'm heading to my hotel room. I'm going to look up some stuff and see what I can find. Is there anything else you can do? Someone on your end that you can ask for help? We can't just sit by and do nothing."

Miko shook his head. "Are you kidding me? You know what I do. I don't exactly hang around in those brainy circles. Wait." He stopped. "The girl. She brought in a new girl to watch over Mr. Campanos, keep him calm and all that. She's another one of those things. She sings."

With a groan, Steve replied, "Great, another unknown. I'll see what I can find. You talk to her and see if you can get anything out of her. Try to make it seem like you want to protect him. Anything to get some information. Call me if you get something," he said as he clicked off the call. He pulled into the parking lot of his hotel, determined to at least win back some favor. He was not ready to leave things how they ended with Haydeez.

Chapter 24

Pandora's siren sat beside the Chimera and stroked his cheek. "Soon you will have everything you desire, everything a creature of your strength deserves," she purred. "You will show everyone what it means to have power. They will cower before your greatness. None will have the supremacy to defeat you."

The Chimera rubbed against her fingertips. A soothing calmness flowed throughout his body. All of the counterparts relaxed as her words poured over them. The serpent's head lay quietly in the siren's lap, eyes closed. The Chimera purred contentedly.

A soft knock pulled the siren away. She lifted the serpent's head and gently placed it on the floor. Without a word, she rose from her seat and walked to the door. The soft click of the knob was the only sound in the dark room. She walked into the hallway and closed the door behind. "May I help you, sir? My brother is sleeping at the moment, dreaming of future conquests no doubt."

Miko nodded. "Would you mind if we spoke in private? It's regarding the safety of Mr. Campanos." He motioned down the hall. "It'll only take a few moments."

The siren nodded and motioned for Miko to lead the way.

Once in a quiet room, he sat in a chair and sighed. "I am concerned about the safety of my employer and I come to you to ask if there is anything I should look out for to ensure he remains protected. As you know, he is no longer himself. In his former body, I knew how to properly protect him from potential threats. But now, I don't know the strengths or weaknesses of his new body. I cannot properly protect him or his family without knowing what needs protecting," he said.

The siren smiled sweetly. "It is unnecessary for you to be concerned, sir. My brother is well protected on his own. His skin is as impenetrable as a Nemean lion, and the fire that currently burns in his belly will easily vanquish his enemies. It is true that he was stopped once before but there are none who are strong enough to aim the iron arrow of Bellerophon and strike with precision. He will be triumphant. You have nothing to fear, sir." She swayed slightly as she spoke. "Do you have other concerns that I may assuage? I will be happy to address them before I return to my brother."

Miko shook his head. "No, I think that's all. I just wanted to make sure we had an understanding regarding the safety and protection of my employer and his family." He stood up. "Thank you for your time."

She smiled and bowed her head. "Of course. Anything to ensure the comfort and bliss of those around me." She turned and quietly left the room. Her body practically floated above the floor. The only thing she left behind was the slight scent of the sea.

Miko left the room and made his way out of the building. He wanted to get as far away from her as possible right now.

•   •   •

Steve fumbled with the phone. It flipped back and forth between his hands as he tried to get a grip on it. He finally held it securely in his hand and pressed the screen. "Did you find anything?" he said without saying hello.

"Good evening to you, Mr. Osbourne. I'm doing well. Thank you for asking. We're never too busy to ignore pleasantries and manners, Mr. Osbourne," Miko said politely. "Now, to answer your question, I believe that I have found some information that will assist you in your ventures. According to the young lady who is currently keeping Mr. Campanos calm and preventing him from destroying everyone around him, whatever he is can be stopped with an iron arrow from Belle phone or something like that."

"Bellerophon? Did she say Bellerophon?" Steve asked.

"That would be correct," Miko answered. "She said it took an iron arrow but there's nobody strong enough to shoot it. So, even if we find this arrow we won't be able to use it."

Steve sighed. "No, there has to be a way to use it. As long as I know there's a way, I'll find someone to use it. I'll let you know when I get it. We'll need to know where he is. Thanks for the info. It'll definitely be put to good use."

Miko took a deep breath and let it out slowly. "I've never thought of doing anything against Mr. Campanos during my entire employ. He's been good to me. He's taken care of me. We're family." He sighed.

Steve shook his head. "It's not him anymore. Just keep focused on that. He let his desires get the better of him and made a really bad choice. Now he's lost forever. There's nothing left for us to do but stop him, Miko. We have to stop him."

"I'll be waiting to hear back from you. Make it quick," Miko said as he ended the call.

Steve let out a breath and groaned. "Now to see if she'll talk to me again. This is going to be fun," he mumbled sarcastically.

Chapter 25

The whistle of a tea kettle pierced the silence in the kitchen. Linx pulled the kettle from the burner and turned off the heat. He poured two cups and put it back on a cold burner. "Trust me. You'll like it. I've never lead you in the wrong direction when it comes to food," he said with a smile. "Just give it a few minutes."

Haydeez chuckled. "I think that's why I like coffee more. I don't have to wait for it to be ready for me. I pour it. I drink it."

Linx sighed. "Just trust me." He handed her a cup with a string hanging over the side. "You forget that I know what you like and don't like and I wouldn't give you something that you'll hate."

"Except that one time..." she started with a smile.

"One mistake! I made one mistake, and I learned from that. But this isn't the same, so you have nothing to worry about, love," Linx answered. "You're never going to forget that are you?"

Haydeez chuckled. "Fine. But just know that I won't be giving up my coffee any time soon."

Linx rolled his eyes and sighed. "I know. I know."

She picked up the cup but before she could take a sip, the gate buzzer sounded from the front door. They locked eyes. "Are we expecting anyone?" she asked, brow furrowed.

"Not that I know of," Linx answered.

They stood up in unison and walked to the door together. The buzzer went off again. "Hello?" said a voice from the speaker.

"Is that..." Linx started.

Haydeez jammed the button down. "What do you want?" Haydeez said, anger in her voice. "I thought we were done."

The speaker crackled. "I need to talk to you. I think I can help with everything. There's someone working closely with my former employer. He was able to provide me with some valuable information. Please. I want to make it up to you. Just let me help and then you can decide if you want to see me again." Steve stared into the camera. "Please. I swear I just want to help."

Haydeez looked at Linx. He threw up his hands, shook his head, and turned around. "Your decision, love."

She smacked her head against the wall a couple times and growled. "I'm giving you ten minutes," she said into the speaker. "If you don't have anything for me, I'll feed you to my goat. He likes trash." She pushed the button to open the gate. "I hate myself."

Linx laughed. "Looks like you're the only one, love."

•   •   •

"Timer's started," Haydeez said as she motioned Steve inside. "This better be worth it." She turned and walked to the living room.

Steve looked at Linx and followed Haydeez inside. "I know you don't want to see me. So, thank you for even answering, let alone opening the door again." Haydeez tapped her wrist. "Right, so, there's a guy in Boston, he's basically the Chimera's right hand man. He found out a way to take down the Chimera."

Haydeez eyed him warily. "So, the guy that's paid to protect him just told you how to kill him? Sounds a bit off to me. How do we know he's telling the truth?" she asked as she crossed her arms.

"He wants him stopped too. He said the guy made a deal with that little girl you said was Pandora and now he's lost inside this thing. He said there's almost nothing left of what the guy used to be and the only way to stop him is to kill him," Steve answered. "He said Stavros dragged his wife and son into this and now they're all inside it, fighting, losing themselves more and more every day. It got so bad that he had to bring in someone to keep him calm."

Haydeez flopped onto the couch. "Ok, so how do we know the info is real? Where did he get it from? Because let's be honest, I really doubt he knows anything about killing a Chimera. He had to ask someone. Who did he ask?"

Steve sat on the edge of the couch. "That girl, Pandora, made a siren. He said it's the thing that is keeping Stavros calm. The siren told Miko the only thing that will kill the Chimera. Miko told her he wanted to make sure he knew what he needed to do to protect Stavros because that's his job. She said there was no need to worry, that the skin is like some kind of lion. You can't pierce it will bullets or a knife or anything. The only thing that will kill it is an iron arrow from…" he paused as he searched in his pocket for a piece of paper. He read the paper aloud slowly, "Bellerophon? I think that's how you say it. As I'm saying this, I'm wondering exactly how insane I sound. If I heard myself, I would start looking for a strait jacket and the nearest hospital. I don't see how you can do this every day and not get fazed by it."

"You have to be a little off to do this job," Linx said. He turned to Haydeez. "Do you think she meant a Nemean lion?"

"Yes!" Steve yelled. "That's what he said. He said it was impenetrable."

Haydeez leaned forward. "Then how will an arrow work if nothing can pierce the skin?"

Steve turned to face her. "You have to shoot it into his mouth. The fire that this thing shoots out of its mouth is hot enough to melt iron. The arrow will melt down its throat and kill it." He shook his head. "It sounds absolutely crazy but so does the rest of this. Look, I feel awful about, well, everything. I just wanted the chance to fix it, or at least help with what I can."

Haydeez looked at Linx. "What do you think?"

Linx shrugged. "If it's true and we go out there with nothing more than the usual arsenal, we're screwed. All I know is that we need to stop it before one of those disasters happens."

With a nod, Haydeez stood up. "So, where do we find this arrow of Bellerophon? I assume it's not just something I can pick up at the local sporting goods store."

Steve stood up as well. "It's a solid iron arrow. I'm guessing it's probably somewhere hard to get to in some remote location. That's how these things work usually, right?"

Linx and Haydeez looked at each other again. "Greek ruins?" they said together.

Chapter 26

The siren sat on the floor with the Chimera's head draped across her lap, eyes closed. Her words were barely audible but she sang a song to soothe the massive creature. She ran her fingers through the fluffy mane. The serpent's head slid up the creature's back and over the horned head like a jealous puppy. She continued her song as the serpent nuzzled under the siren's chin.

"I see they're remaining calm," Pandora said cheerfully. "He will be happy to know that I no longer need him to stay in here. I know that he wants to be outside in the sun, planning his attack on the ones he despises. He will be able to do as he pleases now." She clapped her hands together. "Isn't that wonderful?"

The siren put her fingers under the Chimera's chin and lifted its eyes to hers. "Do you hear that brother? You are now free to plan your attack. What do you desire?" she asked.

"Death," he growled slowly. "Destruction. Total annihilation of my enemies," he purred.

Pandora smiled. "There is no reason to wait any longer. Where do you want to start?"

Miko stood outside the door and listened as his boss took the last step over the edge. He sighed and walked away. There was nothing he could do for Mr. Campanos at this point. He walked out of the building to make a call.

The Chimera stood up and stretched. The serpent swung its head around to look him in the eyes and said, "Think before you act. We must be sure that we will properly strike fear where it is needed." With a wave of the hand, he brushed aside what was left of his wife. She hissed. "Do not dismiss me. I am a part of you now. You will hear me." She snapped her jaws in his face. He struck her and threw her head back against the wall.

"Don't speak to me that way!" he shouted. "I am in control!"

·   ·   ·

"It's me. He's going to be making his move soon. If you've got a plan, I suggest you get it in motion soon," Miko said. "I don't know how long he'll wait before he starts going crazy and setting the whole town on fire."

Steve shuffled his feet. "We're working on it. I think we've got a location for the arrow." He covered the phone and said something that Miko could not hear. There was silence for several moments. When he came back, he said, "Let me know when he's moving. We'll need to know where to find him when the times comes."

"What's going on?" Miko asked. "Where are you going? You can't go too far. What happens if he starts going after the family? You need to end this. I can only hold him off for so long." He sighed. "I'm already looking suspicious. If I start asking more questions or stepping in the way, I'm going to be on the short list if you get my meaning."

Steve nodded. "I get what you're saying. I can't say how long we're going to be because I don't know." He paused. "Look, I can't tell you what I'm doing or where I'm going because I'm not alone. Someone is helping me do all this but I can't say who it is. You just have to trust that we'll get the arrow and be back to take care of him."

Miko scoffed. "Sure, I'll try to have faith in that."

·   ·   ·

Pandora and the siren stood in the hallway and discussed where the Chimera should strike first when they heard a loud thump. Pandora shook her head. "He is losing control quickly. We must send him out now before he destroys himself." She sighed.

"I have found that men truly only want two things from life: physical pleasure and power. Beyond that, nothing matters to them," the siren said quietly. Her body swayed slightly as she spoke, almost as if to hypnotize an onlooker. There was a constant motion, like the tides. "Aunt Pandora, I must ask. Do you intend to destroy the entire world or just remove the men from it? I am curious because this would cause my demise as well." She cocked her head to the side.

With a wave of her hand, she brushed off the comment. "I am only here to destroy man. Your life is in no danger, child." She moved to the door. "We must move quickly. It appears that they battle if you are no longer present."

The siren nodded in agreement.

Pandora opened the door to find the Chimera in distress. He paced and panted heavily. Saliva dripped from his massive jaws and dropped in quiet plops onto the floor. The serpent's head was draped over the back, eyes closed. The other two sets of eyes darted around the room as if it was in search of something.

"Great Chimera, you seem anxious. How may I help you feel at ease, brother?" the siren asked sweetly. She moved to place a tiny hand on the massive creature but it pulled away. Without flinching, she took another step forward. "Calm, brother. I am here to make you happy."

The Chimera roared and shook the walls. "Don't tell me what to do!" he yelled. "I've been locked up in here, told to be patient. Well, I'm done being patient! You do not control me!" He pounded his fists against the floor. "I'm in control!" he roared again.

"Nobody is taking the power from you, brother. I only want to see you happy," the siren whispered melodically. She spoke the way a parent would communicate with a child. "We only want what is best for you, brother. We are here to make sure you achieve your greatest desires." Her voice remained calm and harmonious.

Pandora stood back and watched as the siren tried to bring the Chimera back from his tirade. She smiled to herself as she knew that it did not matter if he was angry now. Ultimately, his end will come, it needed to come. She had to keep herself under control as a laugh had almost escaped her lips. Her fingertips gently brushed over the golden dial that hung from her neck. *You have no control, creature*, she thought to herself. *That is precisely why I chose you. You will go mad and I will consume your essence. Your end is near.*

The siren reached up as the creature let out a breathy growl. He slumped to the ground in a huff. She caressed its face and hummed. He turned into her fingers and whimpered meekly. She leaned into him and pulled his face close to her chest. His head was the size of her petite body and made her look even more miniscule. She cradled him and continued to hum as his eyes rolled back and ultimately closed. "Poor thing. You have exhausted yourself. Rest now, brother. You will need your strength for what is to come next. Your day is near. Your triumph is assured. Sleep and dream of your victory." She turned to Pandora and whispered. "I cannot continue to stop him. If he does not release something soon, it will consume him and he will destroy us as well. Are we leaving now?"

Pandora nodded. "We are leaving." She walked out the door.

"Do you hear that, brother? It is time," the siren said with a smile. She lifted his head up by the chin and caught his eyes. "It is time."

Chapter 27

"Are you out of your mind?" Linx yelled. "You want to take him instead of me? You'd rather have someone who lied to you, watched you, reported your every move back to some stranger, over me? What is wrong with you?" he threw his arms up in the air and turned around. "I get that you can protect yourself and all but why put yourself in a position like that?"

Haydeez stood with her arms crossed. "He seems to think he can redeem himself. I want him somewhere that I can watch him. And besides, if he tries anything, I can throw him from a cliff and nobody will ever find him. Honestly, why is this even an issue? It's not your decision. I'll be fine. He's not going to hurt me."

Linx wiped his hands down his face and sighed. "Fine. Do what you want, love. I'll just stay here," he said as he walked past her and up the stairs.

As he opened the door, he almost knocked Steve over. Without a word, Linx glared at Steve and headed towards the stairs.

Haydeez came through the door and said, "If you try anything, I will throw you from a cliff into the ocean. Are we clear?" she asked. "I may be small but I'd bet any amount of money that I'm stronger than you and faster than you. This in no way makes things kosher between us. After this is all over, I don't want you around. Get me?"

Steve glanced at Linx and back at Haydeez. "Sure. I get you."

"Yeah you do get her," Linx mumbled a little too loud as he trudged up the steps.

Haydeez rolled her eyes. "We head to the airport as soon as I'm packed," she said and headed up the stairs.

•   •   •

Haydeez sat hunched over a laptop, brow furrowed. She typed something and sat back. "Ok, 1 can find this," she said to herself. The cabin of the plane was quiet except for the sound of the engines as they sped through the clouds. She had multiple windows opened on the screen as she searched for possible locations of the arrow. With a groan of frustration she stretched and rolled her neck. She felt someone's hands on her shoulders. For a moment, she closed her eyes and sighed.

Then, her eyes flew opened and she quickly pushed the hands away. "Forgot it was you," she mumbled. "Don't do that."

Steve jerked his hands back and said, "Sorry. Just trying to help. I have no idea what I'm doing and that's all I could think of to make my presence useful." He moved back to a chair and sat.

She rolled her eyes and turned back to the screen. "There's only one reason you're here. 1 can't have you going back to your boss and telling him what I'm doing. If you're in my sight," she paused and caught his gaze. "1 can kill you at the first hint of danger."

"Seems a bit extreme," Steve said as he turned his head to look out the window. "After all, 1 told you the truth about how we met. 1 never tried to hurt you, either of you. 1 wasn't hired to take you out. 1 was supposed to keep you busy. I'm done with that. 1 never should've taken the job to begin with but, other than being hired, 1 was honest about everything. Nothing else was a lie." He turned around to look back at her. His eyes clear, his face void of expression. "Nothing."

Haydeez scoffed and shook her head. "Don't try to play on my sympathies. 1 have none. You screwed up. You lost. End of story," she said as she went back to the screen and scanned the possible locations again. She let out a long groan which turned into a yell.

There was a click. "Is everything alright, Ms. Blackhawk?"

"It's fine. Just can't figure out where I'm going," she answered.

"If we need to change course, just buzz," the pilot said.

"Thank you." She cleared her throat and cracked her neck again. "Where the hell are you?" she mumbled. Her eyes scanned window after window of information. As she closed each one, she shook her head. She leaned back in her seat and crossed her arms. Her eyes glanced around the cabin in defeat. The plane was headed to Greece with no idea where to start the search.

Then she stopped on the screen again. Her eyes did a double take as she scanned the words in the last paragraph. "In the region of Anatolia, on the southern coast of Turkey," she read aloud. "The *coast* of Turkey. You've got to be kidding me." With a few quick clicks, Haydeez had a new window open. The buzz of a phone call followed.

"Hello, love. Landed already?" Linx answered. Sparks flew as he continued with his work on the other end.

Haydeez smiled at the screen. "Not yet. What do you think of an underwater expedition?"

Linx stopped and pulled off his goggles. His hair swept down across his brow. "Huh. Hadn't thought of that." He turned to the screen. "You think it's under water?"

Haydeez chuckled. "It makes perfect sense. Think about it. Lycia is a coastal city yet nobody has ever discovered anything that has to do with the creature, right? What if it was thrown from the cliffs when it was defeated? An arrow from Belleraphon would pack a pretty nasty punch and could easily have knocked this thing back. Or better yet, what if it had been killed and then Belleraphon threw it into the sea for good measure? Either way, I think it's our best bet," she said with another smile.

Linx nodded. "I can see that. Any idea where to start?" he asked.

"How about the ancient city of Olympos?"

•　•　•

Water splashed against the sides of a boat that sat off the coast of Turkey in the Gulf of Antalya. Haydeez came up to the deck in a wet suit. "Ever been under water?" she asked.

"Not like this," Steve said as he shook his head. "This is a first."

Haydeez handed him a mask. "Well, hopefully you're a fast learner. If not, guess my flight back will be a quiet one. Ten minutes we're going under," she said as she walked away.

"If you'd prefer, I could always stay up here," he said.

She scoffed. "Really? You think I'm ready to trust you up here? I trust my eyes right now and they're telling me you're going under without a tank. Nine minutes." She did a last minute check on her equipment before she strapped the tank on her back. When she turned around, Steve fumbled with the straps as he tried to tighten them. "Wow, you're going to drown," she mumbled.

"What?" he asked.

Haydeez rolled her eyes and walked over to him. "Nothing," she said as she grabbed the clip from his hand and pulled. His body jerked forward and came within a few breaths of her face. She could smell him under the scent of the wetsuit. She paused, her eyes on his chest. Her breath caught in her throat as goosebumps trickled down her back and all the way to her fingertips. She looked up into his eyes. A tiny sigh escaped her lips.

Steve froze. He looked into her eyes. "I... Um..." He tried to speak but the words would not form. He moved a hand towards her face.

In one swift movement, she shook her head and pushed him away. "Let's go. Let's get this over with already," she growled as she spun around. "Time to dive."

Steve shook his head and followed Haydeez to the end of the boat. "What if we can't find it? I mean, how do we even know it'll be there?" he asked.

"We don't," she answered curtly. "We go down and look. It's what I do. I figure it has to be close to the coast. I doubt he flew out to the middle of the ocean and dropped the body out there. If he did, then I guess we're screwed. If not, this is probably where it'll be. In ancient times, the city was right on the coast. So, chances are that he fought the creature right over there. My guess is that it's in some hole down under the water. We're close enough to the coast but far enough out that we may actually find something." She paused. "It has to be there. I don't know where else to look."

He moved to put his hand on her shoulder but stopped. He just stood, hand poised in the air, eyes fixed on the back of her head. "Then I guess it's time to dive," he said.

Haydeez cleared her throat. "Just follow me." She flipped off the end of the boat into the water and disappeared.

Steve pulled his mask down and sighed. "This should be fun," he mumbled. He sat on the edge and dropped himself into the water. He had to move quickly to catch up to her.

Haydeez had clicked on a little light on her shoulder strap to allow her to see everything ahead of her. The cold water brought her back to the task at hand. She embraced it and pushed herself forward. She could feel the energy from the water. Everything around her pulsed with its own power. Her breathing was calm and steady as she floated and searched. She allowed the water to pull her in whatever direction it chose.

Steve tried to keep up. He watched her light bob back and forth like a drunk driver on the road. As soon as he went one way, Haydeez turned and quickly went in a different direction. It looked almost like someone had yanked her back and forth under the waves. He swam quickly up to her and finally caught her before she moved away again. With a confused look in his eyes, he grabbed her by the shoulders and looked at her.

Her pupils had fully dilated and her body just floated in front of him. Even with the light in her face, it looked as if her eyes were focused on something else. Steve shook her body but it just wobbled slowly as her head flopped gently back and forth. He put his hands on the sides of her face. "Haydeez!" he tried to yell through his mask. "Haydeez! Snap out of it!"

A golden mist sparkled in her eyes and then disappeared. Her eyes fluttered. She shook her head and focused on Steve. Her brow furrowed in confusion and pulled away. "It's this way," she said, her voice muffled by the mask. "Let's go." She swam away towards some ruins.

"Are you kidding me?" Steve yelled. "What the hell?" He turned and followed her.

Haydeez floated in front of a broken statue. There was nothing showing who it was or why it was here but her body told her this was it. This was a statue of the great warrior, Bellerophon. In one raised hand, he held a thick metal arrow. After being under the water for more years than she even knew, it was still perfect. No rust, no barnacles, no impurities.

Steve swam up next to her and looked. "Wow, you were right," he mumbled.

She moved towards the statue to examine it. She was not sure how to remove the arrow from the hand. So, instead Haydeez decided to do it the easy way. With all her strength, she held onto the hand and kicked the statue's arm. It took several times to make a mark because the water caused her to move slower. The arm finally broke free with an audible crack. The arrow pulsed and vibrated in her hand. She turned and showed it to Steve with a smile.

He returned her smile. "Let's get the hell out of here," he said. He swam up to her.

She turned and headed back to the surface without a response.

"That's fine. I'm not here or anything," Steve mumbled to himself. "I know you hate me and all, but you don't have to ignore me." He looked at the statue for a moment and turned. His head jerked back. He tried to turn around to see what stopped him but he could not move. "Hey! Hey!" he yelled as he tried to reach behind his back. The more he struggled, the further Haydeez got away.

Steve pulled and twisted until he finally broke free. He turned to look and felt water filling his mask. He grabbed for the oxygen hose and felt the loose end. As he gasped for breath, he kicked his feet and tried to swim towards the surface. His arms flailed as he choked on the water. His eyes grew wide, fear visible on his face.

In one urgent movement, his mask came off and water rushed in to greet his nostrils. His eyes slammed shut. He felt something in his mouth and tried to breath. There was still a little water but he was able to breathe again. He felt a tug as his body moved through the water.

When his head crested the surface he spit out the mouthpiece and coughed up the last of the water. He opened his eyes and blinked several times. He could see the coast in the distance as he was dragged backwards. There was a thud followed by a grunt and a few curses. Then, Haydeez hauled him up to the boat. She dropped him on the deck and screamed.

After she picked up the stone hand and arrow, Haydeez walked away. When she returned, she looked down at Steve and asked, "What the hell is wrong with you? How did you get attacked by a statue and almost drowned? Are you stupid?" She stared at him. "Well?"

Steve coughed again. "No, I'm not stupid and there's nothing wrong with me. Also, I have no idea how the statue attacked me. I turned around and probably got caught on something. Could we not act like I did this to myself? I didn't want to drown. In fact, I would prefer to keep water out of my lungs. But since we're discussing stupid things," he answered as he pulled himself to his feet. "What was that zombie act you pulled down there? You went completely blank. You were unresponsive. When you finally came out of it, you looked at me like I had done something to you. Care to explain?"

Haydeez left to start the boat. "You wouldn't understand. Don't delve into things above your level."

Steve stood dumbfounded for a moment, shook his head, and said, "Are you insane?" he yelled. "Fine! I made a mistake. I was paid to do a job. I should've said no but I didn't. I admit it. I'm trying to fix it now but you won't let me." He threw his arms in the air. "What do you want from me? I'm human! Everything I felt was real. Nothing you say or do will change that. So maybe you should just make up your mind with whatever it is that you plan on doing to me, and get it over with already." He sat down and sighed. "I thought you were going to die down there. I couldn't tell if you were breathing. You looked like you had gone into shock and I didn't know what to do." He looked up at her and added, "Sorry, I got too close."

She rolled her eyes and started the boat. Without a word, the boat rumbled back towards the shore.

• • •

As they pulled up to the dock, a man came out to tie off the boat. By the time they stepped onto the dock, he was done. Haydeez had all their equipment in her arms along with the arrow wrapped up in a large cloth. She spoke to the man for a moment and thanked him for the use of his boat. Without a word, they walked to the rental car.

Before she could drop everything in the trunk, Haydeez heard a familiar voice. "Afternoon, Ms. Blackhawk. Fancy meeting you here," the voice said.

She turned around to see a man and woman. "Well hello, Agents. Didn't expect to see you here but, surprise, here you are. To what do I owe this pleasure?" she asked before she turned back around to drop everything in the open trunk. She reached around her back and grabbed the zipper on her wetsuit.

"Well, we just happened to be in the area and when we found out you were here, we figured we would say hello," Agent Blue answered. "So how is the 'vacation' going, Ms. Blackhawk? Enjoying the sights?" she asked sarcastically.

"Always," Haydeez answered with a smile. She dropped her wetsuit on the ground with a plop. She stood in nothing but a two-piece swimsuit that left little to the imagination. With her hands on her hips, she added, "Are you following or did you just want to see how the rich live it up?" she asked with a smirk.

Agent Red cleared his throat. "Classified."

Haydeez chuckled. "Well that's no fun." She turned and grabbed clothing from the car. "So, are you planning on detaining me or just asking veiled questions and reading from a secret file again? I mean, I love a good mystery but what is this really about? I have more important things to do right now."

Confusion crossed Steve's face but he kept his questions to himself. He just stood by the car and listened, happy to be ignored by these strangers. As he took off his wetsuit, he noticed the chill in the air and wondered how Haydeez was able to stand out there in so little. He made a mental note to ask her later, whether she wanted to talk to him or not.

Agent Blue smiled. "Just curious if you were enjoying the scenery with your new boy-toy," she answered. She extended her hand to Steve. "Agent Blue. And you are?"

Before he could answer, Haydeez stepped in and said, "Not important. And we were just leaving. So, once again, if you'll excuse me, I'd like to get to my flight. It's been a pleasure, Agents. Maybe next time you call a girl before you just show up unannounced. I would hate to be ill-prepared for you." She slammed the trunk. With her eyes fixed on the agents, she said, "Get in," and walked away. "We're leaving."

Steve smiled and silently got into the passenger side of the car and closed the door. He glanced in the side mirror as they drove away. "So, are you going to tell me why I'm probably on some weird government watch list for being seen in your company? Wait, I'll answer that for you. 'It's none of your business.' Is that right?" he asked with too much brashness in his voice.

Haydeez slammed on the brakes. "Do you want to be part of this world? Probably not. You had no idea that this even existed until you met me. There is so much more going on right now. You don't know what it takes to do what I do. The less you know, the less likely you'll get me killed in the process," she growled and started to drive again.

"Get you killed? Are you completely insane? You're the one who insists that I stick close to you. You're the one who keeps bringing me back into everything. Do you think I enjoy this? I have no idea what's out there now! Even as a kid, I never really believed in that stuff. Now I find out it's actually all true? And you think that *I'm* the problem?" he yelled. "You are certifiable, you know that?" He put his arm over his eyes and leaned back in his seat. "Wake me when I can go back home."

Haydeez stared at the road. Anger rolled off her body in waves.

Steve could feel the tension in the air and snuck a peek. Haydeez gripped the steering wheel. Her eyes never moved from the road ahead. He was aggravated and frustrated and wanted nothing more than to just go home but there was something that kept him there. It was not because she told him to come. There was something about her that made him want to stay. He could not explain it. She was not very personable and had a hell of a temper but he found it difficult to pull himself away from her.

"I thought there was going to be a kraken or something guarding the arrow," he said quietly as he cleared his throat.

"What?" Haydeez snapped.

Steve sat up. "In the water, I thought there was going to be some kind of weird sea monster that tried to eat us or something. I mean, after the creepy snake lady and then the fox thing and finding out my boss is a three-headed animal, I figured something else had to be there."

"There isn't always something trying to kill me," she scoffed. "Actually, now that you mention it, there usually is something that wants to kill me. I usually have to trap it or kill it." Her body relaxed. "Most of the time I'm just hired to get rid of something. They tell me where it is and then I go get it. Weird," she said to herself.

Steve smiled and added, "But at least you know what you're doing. I'm flying blind here. I have no idea what's going on and I don't know if I ever will. This is all completely insane to me. I keep looking over my shoulder, thinking something is just going to pop up and start chasing me. How do you deal with this every day?" He took the opportunity to try to get her to talk. Anything to break the thick tension that began to suffocate the car.

"It's really not that bad," she answered. "Most creatures aren't really out to kill you. They just want to live. Think of them like cats or horses or..." she paused. "Big, goofy dogs that only want to play." She sighed. "Ugh, I hate Peter," she mumbled to herself.

Steve cleared his throat. "So, what's up with the suits? I take it you know them too. Seems like they already have answers but wanted to see how much you actually know," he said.

She rolled her eyes. "Met them not too long ago when I was finishing up something up in Ireland. I don't know what they're doing but they seem to know who I am and what I'm doing. So far they've kept their distance in a fight but who knows how long that's going to last. Which reminds me..." She pulled out her phone and dialed. "Hey, guess who I ran into?" she asked.

"Who was there?" Linx asked on the other end of the line.

"Our colorful agent buddies. They were asking what I was doing here, like they don't already know. I mean, they have to be watching me. Not that I care. What are they going to do? Stop me from saving the world?" she chuckled.

Linx groaned. "I'll do a little more digging, see if I can find anything out about them. Is everything else alright?" he asked tentatively.

"I'm behaving myself," Steve said. "I haven't tried to take advantage of her or anything."

"Not what I meant but thanks for the update, mate," Linx answered. "Do we have it?"

Haydeez smiled. "We've got it."

Linx sighed. "You are amazing, love. You're headed for the plane, right?"

"Of course."

"I'll see you when you get back, love."

Steve glanced back and forth between Haydeez and the phone after she hung up. He tried to stay quiet but inside he wanted to know. "So, what's up with you two? I mean, it's obvious that he likes you but either you don't notice it or don't care."

"And that's your business because?" she asked. "Linx is one of the only people I trust. You're not on that list. That's all you need to know." She paused. "Are we done with the questions now? And by the way, do you think it could be possible to keep your hands to yourself on the flight back?"

Steve nodded. "Sure, if you can help me understand a few things. For one, how the hell were you able to stand out there in the cold in nothing but a few strips of fabric? I mean, I took off my wetsuit and my teeth started chattering. What the hell?"

Haydeez glanced at him. "A few things?"

"Ok, I thought there would be something guarding that arrow but there wasn't. Not only was there nothing guarding it but there was nothing in the water at all. No fish, no sharks, no sea life whatsoever. Why?" he asked.

"Is that all?" Haydeez asked.

Steve hesitated. "Actually it's not. Why am I here, and what do you plan on doing with me? There's really no reason for me to be here. I'm more afraid of what you'll do to me than what my boss will do to me if he finds out what I told you about him. So, why are you keeping me around?"

Haydeez sighed. "The cold thing, no idea. I just don't feel it like everyone else does I guess. I mean, I get cold and stuff but I guess it depends on the kind of cold. When it's snowing, I'm done but a little breeze doesn't even faze me." She paused. "As far as there not being anything guarding the arrow, again, I have no idea. I didn't even notice. It's like the arrow wanted to be found. I swear I heard it call me. Like right now, I can hear it thanking me for saving it. I mean, it's not like us talking but..." she paused. "It's more like a feeling of relief that I feel but it's not my relief. I don't really know how to explain it."

With his eyes wide, Steve just listened. He had no idea what to say.

"And as far as what I plan to do with you, at this point I'm pretty much making it up as I go but I can't let you leave and tell your boss what I'm planning. So, basically we're at an impasse," she added with a sigh.

They sat in silence for several moments. The only sound was the hum of the engine.

"Hold on. Didn't that arrow kill this thing once already?" Steve asked.

"Yeah, why?" Haydeez answered.

Steve tilted his head to one side. "Then how do we have a fully formed solid iron arrow wrapped up back there if it already melted?"

Haydeez scoffed. "Because..." she started. "It..." she tried again. She hit the brake. "I need to call someone." Her fingers raised over the buttons on her phone.

Steve laughed. "You don't know? You mean, you don't have an answer to something?"

She shot him a dirty look. "Hey, it's me. I need some info."

"Are we just going to sit here in the middle of the road and wait for someone to hit us?" Steve said as he looked around. He caught her eye again and flinched. "Nevermind."

"It's nobody," she answered, eyes still on Steve. "I need to know why the iron arrow that originally killed the Chimera and supposedly melted down its throat is now whole again in the trunk of my rental. I need to know I have the right thing before I go after him." She paused and listened.

Cornelius sighed. "That's an interesting question. Do you have some time to wait? I'll have to do research."

Haydeez nodded. "I don't have a lot of time but go ahead. I need to know if I have the right thing." She headed down the road again. "I'm on my way back to the airstrip. How long do you think it will be?" she asked.

Cornelius cleared his throat. "Well dear, it all depends on how long it will take to find the information you seek. Perhaps you could give me a little more detail about where you found this arrow."

"It was in the hand of a statue of Bellerophon under water," she answered quickly. "It was off the coast. There were a bunch of ruins in the water. The arrow was clean."

"What do you mean by clean?" Cornelius asked.

"No water damage. No barnacles. Not a hint of rust," Haydeez answered. "Those ruins have been there for centuries and that arrow looked like it was dropped in this morning. It has to be right." She paused. "It called me."

Cornelius stopped. "It called you?" he asked tentatively.

With a sigh, she started. "Ok, so, it didn't talk to me like we're talking now. It was different. It was like a song almost. There was a whisper as soon as I hit the water. I followed it through the water. It pulled me to the ruins."

"I see," Cornelius answered. Pages fluttered as he flipped through the book on his table. "Is this something you experience often? This whisper, do you hear it at other times as well?"

"I have, yes. It sometimes happens when I'm near magic or mystically charged things, like the arrow," she said. "If there's too much around me I get an almost drunk sensation. That's really the only way to describe it."

Steve stared at her as his brow furrowed. "Is that what happened in the water?" he whispered.

Haydeez glanced at Steve and nodded.

Cornelius sighed. "You become more interesting every time we speak, dear." He cleared his throat. "I don't believe you need my help as much as you think. It sounds to me like you already know the arrow is real. Is it speaking to you now, dear? What is it telling you?"

A slight gasp escaped her lips. "It was forged again." She moved the car off to the side of the road and parked it. "It's showing me images of when it was forged after the Chimera was killed the first time. It's like a movie replaying over and over. Little pulses coming off it." She put her hand on the door to steady herself. "Why is it doing this? It's like that thing can understand me or something."

"In my experience I've found that items like your arrow want to be found. They don't necessarily have a mind of their own but they have their own energy and they push it out for someone to find," Cornelius answered. "Think of those times you've felt like someone was watching you. That may have actually been an item trying to reach out to you and you just didn't realize it. If someone is what I like to call 'sensitive', they tend to feel these things more frequently and stronger. You, dear, are beyond 'sensitive'. You are your own category altogether."

Haydeez let out a steady breath. "Lucky me, I suppose. At least I know this is the right thing." She cleared her throat and turned her attention back to the road. "We have to get back to the plane. I need to get home."

Chapter 28

The wind rushed past the windows of the plane as it headed out over open waters. "Ok, now that you've got the arrow, can I go home?" Steve asked from his seat. "I'm pretty sure it will make all those involved a little happier."

Haydeez rolled her eyes. "Like I said, we're not done yet. Once that thing is dead, you're free to go, unless you want to fight me." She turned around to face him. "How about it? You want to try?"

Steve sighed. "Fine. What else do we need to do? I'd love to get away from you as soon as possible."

"Excuse me? You're the one that started all this. You came to find me. Then, when I made you leave, you came back. So, if you really wanted to go, you've had plenty of chances. Let's not pretend like I'm holding you captive or anything," Haydeez answered. "You chose to be around me. I just wanted to make sure I could see you at all times, so I know exactly what you're doing."

Steve scoffed. "So, it's like a 'know your enemy thing', he said sarcastically.

"Exactly," she answered.

"Except we're not enemies!" he yelled. "We're fighting for the same thing. I don't understand why you can't see it. I didn't ask to be in this world but I'm along for the ride. So stop acting like a damn harpy and accept the help when it's offered!"

Haydeez stood up. "A harpy? Who do you think you are?"

Steve stood up as well. "What about you? You walk around like you know everything and everyone should bow down to your knowledge and expertise. Your little friend back home seems to be content taking orders but that's not how I do things. I came back because I realized what was actually happening and I wanted to stop it. My employer went nuts. He's some weird lion, snake, goat thing now and I have no idea how that's even possible. He's not human anymore! I'm freaking out here!" he yelled.

She moved towards him. "You're on *my* plane! You don't talk to me like that!" she answered. She moved to swing at him. As she pulled her arm back the plane bounced. Haydeez stumbled a little.

The speaker box dinged. "My apologies, Ms. Blackhawk. It looks like we're hitting some turbulence. Please take a seat and strap in," the pilot said.

As the plane continued to bump, Haydeez lurched forward and fell. She caught Steve on the leg and pulled him down. They tumbled to the floor in a heap. Haydeez groaned and rolled over. Steve was thrown across her stomach. "Get off," she said through gritted teeth.

He pushed himself off her and crawled to his chair. As he climbed up into the seat, he heaved an audible sigh. After he secured himself, he looked at Haydeez and said, "Look, I don't know what I'm doing and I'm trying to stick with the one person who seems to be the most calm in all of this. I want to survive and if that means staying close to you, then that's what I intend to do for as long as possible."

Haydeez sighed. "Fine. I get it. I was born into this. You weren't. It's just very hard to get past trust issues. I like things a certain way and when they change, I don't handle it very well." She cleared her throat. "I'm not going to let you die, unless I kill you myself and I'm not going to promise that I won't do that." She smiled and added, "I'm trying to get through this alive, same as you."

"Did you just say something nice to me?" Steve laughed. "Careful Ms. Blackhawk. You might be showing a heart."

Haydeez leaned back in her chair and chuckled, "Can't let that happen. Better be more careful next time."

•   •   •

Haydeez opened the front door and yelled, "I'm home!" She knocked snow off her boots and stepped inside. "Make sure you take yours off and leave them right here. I hate wet floors." She pointed to a spot as she walked in and kicked her boots into a cubby.

Steve followed and left his large boots in another opening. He helped her off with her jacket and shared a smile.

Linx called from the other room. "Great timing. I just finished dinner. Oh good, we're all friends again," he added as he rounded the corner. With an irritated sigh, he forced a smile and motioned to the dining room.

Haydeez lifted the arrow with a chuckle. "Check it out," she said. "Now we just need to find him and take him out before he hurts anyone."

Steve quickly reached into his pocket and pulled out his phone. "Oh! I've got that covered," he said with a smile. "Give me just a minute." He turned around and made a quick call.

Linx eyed Haydeez. "So, what's going on? I thought you were done with him. Now you're best friends or something?"

"Relax. We've just come to an agreement," she said. "It doesn't make sense for us to be fighting when we're all trying to get to the same point in the end. It's not a race. Teamwork, right?" She bounced happily into the dining room.

Steve came up to Linx with a smile. "Done. I know where he is. Just have to get there now," he said as he put his hand on Linx's shoulder. "Great news, huh?"

"Don't touch me, mate. I don't know what you did, but I still don't like you. I don't like liars," Linx answered. "Food's getting cold," he added and walked away.

Steve shook his head and followed Linx.

Chapter 29

Thunder rumbled through the grey clouds that hung low over Lappland. The wind whipped around Pandora as she held the Phenix egg over her head. Her eyes fluttered and she chanted in a language no longer native to any country in the world.

In the distance, a woman walked toward Pandora. Her legs seemed stiff and jerked with each step. She turned her head to the side to avoid what was in front of her. Her red hair spun around her face in a flurry of tendrils. The wind pounded her back and easily commanded her to continue.

Pandora smiled as the woman grew near. The wind began to spread. It created an area much like the eye of a hurricane. Around her body was nothing but calm. Within a few steps in any direction, debris spun past at terrifying speeds. "You are here," Pandora said happily. "Welcome, daughter."

The woman stopped inside the calm. "Who are you?" she asked. Her brow furrowed as her eyes darted back and forth. "Why am I here?" She bit her lip and rubbed her arms.

Pandora giggled. "The egg has called you home. It is your time. You have returned to your birthplace and now we can move forward. You have nothing to fear, daughter. Together, we will end man as was intended from my creation."

Tears welled up in the woman's eyes. "What? What are you talking about?" she asked with a tremble in her voice. "I don't want to be here. I don't want to kill anyone. Please, just let me go," she begged.

Pandora shook her head. "But you are a part of this. You must stay. Not to worry. You do not have to take a life. They will be taken on your behalf." Pandora smiled. "Yours and your brother's."

The woman shook her head. "I don't have a brother and I have no idea who you are." She gripped the sides of her head and closed her eyes. "I want to go home. I want to go home!" she yelled and dropped to her knees. "Let me go!"

"Everything will be clear soon, daughter."

•　　•　　•

Screams echoed between the buildings in South End as the Chimera moved down the street. People ran in every direction. The creature moved at a leisurely pace towards the harbor. Its eyes focused forward. "Now we show them all what we're capable of," the creature growled through gritted lion teeth. "It's time for them to know fear." With its head thrown back, it let out a growl that vibrated the windows of nearby vehicles.

"They will understand soon enough, brother. All your enemies will reek of terror," the siren brushed against the Chimera's massive arm. "See how these strangers run from you. Taste what they're feeling. Breathe it in, brother," she purred.

The Chimera took a deep breath. A heavy rumble began low in its belly. He laughed. "Run if you must, feeble humans. You will all be casualties. Your death will be exhausting for you." The ground began to shake with each step he took. Debris fell from the buildings all around him. "No more waiting. No more holding back," he said. He raised his arms out to his sides as the serpent head weaved around behind him. It hissed and spat on the ground.

"Now it's my time! Fear me!" he yelled. His roar shattered the windows of a nearby car.

"Fear me!"

Explosions sounded all around.

"Fear me!"

Screams echoed into the night as the aftershocks subsided.

Chapter 30

Linx stared daggers at Steve as the unwelcomed guest laughed with Haydeez. With his arms crossed, he leaned back in his chair and watched. He listened to them chat and giggle as they ate dinner and drank their wine. It was as if they had known each other for years. Inside, the only thing he could think of was if his fork would go all the way through Steve's hand or if the bone would stop it. But instead he stood up and said, "Well, I'm just all laughed out." He picked up his plate and began to walk to the kitchen. "I'll be cleaning up and heading to bed then."

Haydeez sighed. "Yeah, we probably should be heading to bed too. We're leaving first thing in the morning. I want to stop this thing as quickly as possible, you know, before it goes on some kind of killing spree."

Steve chuckled. "Little late for that don't you think. I mean he is a mob boss and all."

"Ha ha. I know that," Haydeez chuckled. "You know what I mean."

They stood in unison and laughed.

Linx stood at the sink and rinsed a dish as they walked in the kitchen. Haydeez placed her dishes in the sink and said, "That was great. Thanks for dinner, Linx." Her fingers brushed his shoulder and she smiled.

"Yeah, that was great," Steve chimed in and smacked Linx on the back. "Might have to eat here more often."

Linx rolled his eyes. His nose twitched before he spoke. "Hands off, mate," he growled.

Steve chuckled. "Something wrong?" he asked.

"You don't want to go there, mate," Linx said with his eyes in the sink.

"Maybe I do, *mate*," Steve answered with a sneer. "If you've got a problem with me, spit it out. Get it over with. I'm standing right here. I can take it."

Linx took a deep breath and let it out slowly. "Out of respect for *my friend*, I think I'll just step back. After all, I'm not about to spill your blood in her kitchen." He lifted his head and added, "Just remember, she's the only reason."

Steve laughed. "You think you can take me, computer boy. Maybe we should move this outside so you can try. You have no idea what you're getting yourself into."

Haydeez stepped in and said, "Hello, does anyone even care what I think? You know, my house and all that."

Linx shut off the water and turned around, fire behind his eyes. "Like I said, love, you're the only reason." He shook water off his hands in Steve's direction and walked past him.

Steve scoffed. "Kind of childish don't you think?" he called after Linx. He followed Linx out into the living room where the warmth of the fireplace flooded the room. "You just don't get it, do you?"

Linx stopped and turned. "What don't I get, mate? Why don't you share with all of us? What don't I get?" he asked as he spread his arms wide. "Enlighten the room."

"You're not good enough. You're not man enough. You're not enough. Period," he said through gritted teeth. "There's nothing about you that she dreams about. You're the brother she has to take care of, not the man she wants to be with." He stepped up to Linx. With their eyes locked, he lowered his voice barely above a whisper and added, "You're an obligation, not a lover, and you'll never be one."

Linx balled up his fist and swung hard. He connected with Steve's cheek as a thud sounded.

Steve laughed and swung back. His fist hit Linx in the stomach.

Linx fell forward and gasped as he tried to catch his breath. He went head first into Steve to knock him off balance. They were a jumble of fists as each tried to take down the other.

Haydeez watched for a moment, unable to decide if she was flattered at the display or insulted that they would do this in her home. She quietly stepped over to the Harley as it sat silently on its kickstand. She hopped on and grabbed the clutch. The bike roared to life. She pulled back on the throttle and revved the engine for a second.

The two men stopped to look at her, surprise apparent on their faces.

Her eyes narrowed. She shut off the bike and climbed off. "In my house," she said calmly. "My home." She started to walk slowly towards to men. "My refuge from all the anger and hate and pettiness out there. I expect more. I expect respect." She stood a few feet from them. Her small frame did nothing to diminish her intimidating stare. "I make my own decisions. I choose who enters these walls. Nobody comes in without my approval. Is that understood?" she asked.

"I'm sorry. I understand," Linx said as he pulled himself up.

Steve looked at him with a smile and a chuckle.

Haydeez scoffed. "I take it you don't understand, Steve," she said as she cocked her head to the side. "Or do you just not care?"

Steve cleared his throat and answered, "I understand."

Haydeez crossed her arms. "I kind of thought we were all adults but I guess some of us are not even human. Only animals fight over Alpha status. You both want to act like angry animals, well guess what? I'm the Alpha here. Who wants to step up and fight the Alpha for control, hmm? Who wants to be first?" she asked.

Both men stood up straight and dusted themselves off but neither wanted to make a move towards her.

"That's what I thought. I have had enough of this." She turned to face Steve. "You, Linx has been in my life and by my side for more years than I remember. He has been my right hand and my partner. He's backed me up and stood by my side in more dangerous situations than a normal friend would tolerate. He's more important to me than you need to know." She turned to Linx. "And you, after everything we've been through, you turn into a jealous child when another boy chases me around the playground. We're best friends but you need to let me try to be happy. Let me make mistakes. Let me fall. I'm not delicate. I won't break if someone hurts me." She walked over to Linx and put her hands on his shoulders. "You don't need to protect me."

He looked into her eyes, all the anger gone. The only thing that remained was sadness. "It's not that. I want you to be happy but it has to be with someone you can trust, not someone who is willing to lie to you from the moment you meet." He paused for a moment as he stared into her eyes. "And yes, I do need to protect you. It's not about possession or happiness. You're not invincible, love. Do you not remember what happened just a short while ago? You still have a slight scar in spite of how quickly he healed you. You try to save everyone else like some kind of super hero or something. Did you ever think that maybe sometimes it's ok to let someone save you?" He sighed. "Good night," he said as he turned and walked up the stairs.

Without a glance in his direction, she said, "You should go too, Steve. I don't think I need help on this one." Her voice sounded somber. "I've got what I need. I don't need you around anymore."

Steve took a deep breath and sighed. "Fine. I'll go. But you know where to find me."

As the front door closed, Haydeez heaved a heavy sigh of her own. She dropped to the floor and stared into the fireplace. Her eyes followed the flames as they fluttered and danced along the logs. With each wisp of smoke that disappeared up the chimney, she counted until her body finally released the tension. Her mind became lost in the energy and warmth and she began to sway. Her heartbeat pulsed in time with the flicker of the flame. Her muscles relaxed into the rhythm of the dance. The fire spoke to her, called to her, calmed her.

Chapter 31

Haydeez awoke as Linx shook her and yelled her name. "What happened? Why are you on the floor?" he asked, his voice breathy. "Are you alright?"

She pulled herself up and brushed the hair from her face. "I'm fine. What's wrong? Why are you yelling at me?" she asked. Her fingers brushed against the carpet. "I'm in the living room still. Ok, that would be why," she mumbled. She pulled herself up with a grunt. "I guess I was just really tired. I sat down in front of the fireplace and fell asleep." She licked her dry lips and cleared her throat. "Coffee. Food," she added and headed to the kitchen.

"Are you sure you're alright?" Linx asked as he followed. "I've never seen you like this before." He started to pull food from the fridge to make breakfast while Haydeez pressed the button on the coffee pot and the familiar hiss followed.

She pulled some mugs from the cabinet. "I'm fine. Actually, I'm better than fine. I'm calm. I'm relaxed. I feel great." She paused for a moment. "I'm great."

Linx shook his head. He fixed a quick breakfast and sat on one of the barstools. "What time are you heading out?" he asked.

Before she could answer, there were a series of beeps. They both turned to look at a closed laptop. "What is that for?" she asked.

"Probably weather anomalies," he answered with a sigh. "Let's find out." He grabbed the laptop and popped it open. His face drained of all color and his eyes grew wide. "It's not good, love. It's really bad. No, bad would be an understatement. Disturbing." His mouth hung open.

Haydeez pulled the laptop over. Her eyes scanned the images on the screen of fires and devastation. There was video after video of fear as people ran and screamed and cried. "These are from last night. Why are we just now getting these?" she asked.

Linx rubbed his face. "System overload probably. Just the sheer volume of news stories overloaded the alert system and it must have rebooted. This is bad."

She stared blankly at the screen then slammed it shut. "Time to go." She hurried from the room. "Call the airstrip. Tell them I'm on my way. I need to be in the air last night." She stopped for a moment. "There's too many cameras. They'll see me." She looked at Linx. "Someone might have already caught the Chimera."

Linx smiled. "Got you covered, love. I'll pack a little toy I've been working on. With all the chaos Pandora is throwing at us, there was bound to be news coverage. My little buddy will kill electronics nearby so, no cameras, no phones, no pictures of you." He smiled proudly.

"Perfect," she answered. "Get it packed. I'll be right down." She ran up the stairs to her bedroom.

Linx raced down to the basement to pack her gear. Neither one heard the gate intercom buzz. "Hello?" the voice said over the speaker.

After five minutes, they both came back into the living room. Haydeez had thrown on jeans, a long sleeve shirt, and her moccasins. Linx had a small duffle bag packed full of gear. He held out his hand. "When you get out there, press this button. It sends out a signal that will temporarily shut off everything electronic. You'll lose me for a minute or two but I've tweaked your ear piece to reboot quickly. Everything else will take about 20 minutes to come back up. So, be quick."

A buzz interrupted him followed by the same voice again. "Hello?"

Linx rolled his eyes. "Are you ready?"

Haydeez nodded and grabbed her bags. "I'm counting on you to get me to the right place. Once I land, I'll need to know where I'm headed. Watch those news stories. I need to get in and get out as quickly as possible."

"Are you sure you don't want me to come with you? Another body on the ground is not a bad thing. I can help herd the people out of the way," Linx said.

Haydeez looked him in the eyes. "Another body on the ground is not good when the body stops moving. I will feel better if you're here." She pressed the intercom button. "Hello." There was a buzz as she opened the gate. "You are my eyes when I'm out there. Help me see, Linx." She smiled. "Besides, it shouldn't take that much. I've got the arrow. We're good to go. In and out, right? Keep the house warm. I'll be back tonight." She opened the door and walked out.

He walked up behind her and held the door open for a moment. He watched as she climbed into the passenger seat of Steve's car once more. She waved to him, smile on her face and closed the car door. He waved back and stepped into the comfort of the house. As the door closed, he dropped his forehead against it and whispered, "In and out. You better be back tonight."

•   •   •

"And you need to go back to the house. Linx might need help monitoring all those alerts. The system got overloaded and I need to know where I'm going," Haydeez said as she climbed out of the car and grabbed her bags. She nodded at the pilot.

Steve stepped around the car. "But you don't know your way around the city. How will you even know where to go?" he asked.

"Not important. I will find my way. I need eyes here in case something happens. It's not good if the whole world finds out these things are real. I mean just look at how you reacted. I'm surprised you're still here right now," she answered. "Too many people out there running toward this thing and that will draw attention. But one crazy lady, well, people will chalk that up to insanity. Besides, I will not put anyone else in harm's way. I need this thing to focus on me to kill it. I can't give it other targets." She started to walk towards the plane. "Just go back to the house."

Steve ran after her and stepped in front of her. "What if you don't come back?"

Haydeez scoffed. "You don't know me," she smirked. She moved around him towards the plane again.

"Ok, that's true but I still care, and if I send you off alone and something happens, I'll never forgive myself," he added.

"Learn to forgive, Steve," she called over her shoulder. "If you don't it'll hurt your soul."

He stood in the private hanger, mouth open, as he watched her go up the steps. "Wow, nothing will change her mind," he mumbled.

The plane engine roared to life. As the door closed, Steve turned back towards his car. The plane left the hanger and Steve stood with his fingers on the car handle in silence. "I hope this isn't a mistake."

•   •   •

"Me again," Steve said into the speaker box outside the gate. "She asked me to come back and help you."

"What's that, mate? Can't hear you," Linx shouted into the speaker.

Steve sighed. "Whatever. Look, just let me in. I don't want to be here and you don't want me here. But she asked me to come here, so I did. Now just let me in, man."

The box crackled. "As long as you know how unwelcome you actually are,"Linx said. The gate buzzed and opened.

Linx stood at the front door, hands on the door frame, as Steve pulled up and got out. "If you're here with me, that means she went alone. Why did you let her go alone?" he asked angrily.

Steve scoffed. "Let her? You think I let her? You don't know her as well as you think you do." He pushed past Linx into the house. "What are we looking for?" he asked from the living room.

Linx grumbled and rolled his eyes. "I know her better than you do," he mumbled to himself. "Weather. We're looking at weather." He walked into the living room and said, "Basement."

"Wow, you will do anything to say as little as possible to me," Steve answered. He shook his head and walked toward the basement door. "Hate me if you want, but know that I'm not leaving until she tells me to go."

"Brilliant," Linx mumbled. His cell phone rang. "Haydeez? What's happening?"

"I haven't landed yet. We're getting news from the area. We might not be able to land close enough. There's a lot of destruction. We're trying to figure out what to do right now," she said.

Steve came back up the stairs to listen.

"But if you land too far away it'll take too long for you to drive out there and it might be too late. What other options do you have?" Linx asked.

"I don't know. Air drop?" she said jokingly.

"That's not funny, love," Linx said. "The airstrip can't be that damaged. It's just an open piece of land."

Haydeez chuckled. "It might not be funny, but it's an option that I've already discussed with the pilot. He knows that I need to get out there as quickly as possible." She paused. "Look, it's a last resort, ok? If there are no other options, there's still that."

Linx sighed. "And I'm not there to stop you. Bloody brilliant."

Steve's brow furrowed as he mouthed 'What?' and shrugged his shoulders.

Linx waved him off and added, "Keep me posted. And find another way, love. Seriously. You're not some military unit. It's you, alone, and it's not safe."

Haydeez groaned. "I know. We're trying. I'll call you back."

As Linx hung up the phone, Steve said, "Don't brush me off, man. What the hell is going on?"

Linx rubbed his hands over his face and groaned. "She might not be able to land. She wants to drop in."

"What?" Steve yelled.

Chapter 32

Lightning exploded and streaked across the sky followed quickly by the boom of thunder. Windows shook and car alarms blared as the vibrations set off those with sensitive settings. People ran in every direction, some from the weather, most from the Chimera.

The creature that once was Stavros Campanos and his family stood in the middle of the street. Fires burned all around. Embers sparkled in the sky. The Chimera breathed in a mixture of smoke and fear. "We are almost there. We can feel the earth. We feel the heat beneath waiting to explode." He breathed out heavily. "It will be a sight to behold. Everyone will fear us."

"What will you unleash, brother?" the siren asked. She ran her fingers down his arm. "What will you do to your enemies?"

A calm crept through his body and he sighed. "When we reach the water, beneath the waves we will call forth the power of the earth itself. We will awaken the sleeping volcano and rain fire upon this land. Boiling water will fall from the sky. There will be a great explosion beneath the quiet ocean and everyone will know it was us. We will cause massive destruction and it will be glorious!" he yelled as he raised his arms.

The siren slid closely next to him. "I am honored to be at your side, brother. I am humbled to be beside one as magnificent as yourself," she purred. "See the terror you cause in your wake?" she asked, her arm spread out in front of them. She turned to see the flames lick rooftops and reach for the stars above. "It truly is exhilarating, brother." With her eyes focused back on the Chimera, she whispered, "Shall we continue, brother?"

The Chimera roared in response. With each bellow, an earthquake shook the city. Buildings vibrated. Chunks of concrete fell around them but the pair walked arm in arm down the middle of the road as if it were a sunny spring day.

By the time the Chimera could see the water, the city was a cloud of red, orange, and black behind him. Sirens echoed between what was left of the buildings. People screamed. Alarms blared. The Chimera ignored it all and walked.

Across the pike, air traffic controllers argued with a pilot over whether or not they were allowed to land.

"Look, we're running low on fuel. If we don't land now, we'll be crashing. What's it going to be?" the pilot asked.

Several minutes passed as the pilot circled the airfield. Finally, the controller responded. "You have permission to land. Refuel and get airborne ASAP. Boston is in a state of emergency. We've had several earthquakes. The city is on fire. It's not safe for you to be here." His voice crackled over the radio.

"Understood," the pilot responded. "Are we clear to begin our descent?"

Haydeez gently patted the pilot on his shoulder and left the cockpit. She grabbed her bag and buckled her seat belt as the plane began to dip. By the time the wheels touched down she could already smell the smoke in the distance. Before the pilot had a chance to shut off the engine, she was up and at the door. When she felt them stop moving, she yelled to the pilot, "Fuel up and take her to the closest airfield not hit by the fires. I'll call when I'm done."

"You got it, Ms. Blackhawk. Stay safe out there," he responded.

She popped open the door and hopped out of the plane before he even stood up. She raced across the tarmac. "I'm on the ground," she shouted. "We almost couldn't land. He's taking her to the closest strip and I'll drive there when I'm done."

A man with a clipboard met her at a side entrance. "Ms. Blackhawk, your vehicle is waiting for you. Welcome to Boston. I wish we had a more pleasant greeting for you," he said as he held the door open for her. "Please, right this way." He motioned for her to enter.

"Thank you," she said. They walked down a long hallway. The smell of smoke seemed to dissipate the further they got into the building. It was not as strong but it still lingered. "I'll be returning it outside of the city," she said.

The man nodded. "Of course, Ms. Blackhawk. I certainly hope your family is somewhere safe right now. The city is in absolute chaos right now. We've never seen anything like this before," he added quickly with a quiver in his voice.

"They're fine. I've already spoken to them," she responded calmly. "I just want to get out there as quickly as possible and get them out."

"Absolutely, Ms. Blackhawk. Normally, we wouldn't allow such a transaction for anyone other than military or government officials in a state of emergency. However, one such as yourself, commands more... leniency than most others. We like to take care of our 'special' clients whenever possible."

Haydeez chuckled. "You mean people that are swimming in money," she blurted. "I appreciate the accommodations."

As they reached another door, he jumped in front of her and grabbed for the handle. He cleared his throat. "Well, yes, ma'am. Anything we can do to assist you during your stay, rain or shine, or apparently fire and earthquakes," he said with a forced smile. He opened the door and ushered her inside. "Your vehicle is right outside." He handed her the keys and dipped his head slightly.

She grabbed the keys. "Thanks again." She walked through the doorway into baggage claim. The man had taken her through tunnels under the building which led directly to the exit. There were no people in any direction. The building was clear as she ran out the door.

An SUV sat parked right out front. She pressed the alarm button. The lights flashed and the alarm chirped. "I'll be heading across the bridge in a few, Linx." She tossed her bag on the passenger seat and climbed behind the wheel. "Hopefully, I can make it across."

"If you run into any blocks along the way, I tossed something extra in your bag, you know, just in case," he said over her ear piece. "There's a government badge in there. Typically, people don't ask questions when they see one. The bridge is probably blocked off, so you'll most likely need it to cross."

Haydeez unzipped the bag and found the badge right on top of everything. "Aw, you shouldn't have. You always know just what to get me," she said with a chuckle. The SUV pulled out of the terminal. Across the harbor, the sky was red and orange as the fires burned into the night. She sighed. "This is bad, Linx. If you thought jumping from a plane was bad, you should see what I'm looking at right now," she said. Her voice was soft and somber. She turned the video call on her phone and flipped the camera.

At home, in the quiet of the mountains, Linx watched. All he could do was watch. His mouth hung open. The screen showed flames in the distance that tore through buildings like they were tissues. Lights flashed as fire trucks stopped in the middle of the street. Smoke casually floated across the bay. "Bloody hell, love. This thing needs to be stopped. It's going to take down the whole city," he whispered.

"I know. But there's so many people..." she paused. "I can't save everyone, Linx. The city is going to crumble and I can't stop it." She sniffled. "So many people are probably already dead."

Linx swallowed and cleared his throat. "Listen to me, love. Remember the kids you saved from the fox? Remember how grateful they were that you saved them? You can beat yourself up for things that have already happened if you want, but it's not your fault. There are millions of people out there that are counting on someone to stop this. They don't know it's you but they're out there praying to whoever they pray to that someone will make this nightmare end. You will stop him, love," he said. "I know you won't let those people down."

The image flickered as she crossed the bridge. "Linx? I think I'm losing the signal. Something is messing with the service. I'll try you when I find the Chimera." The screen went blank and the call ended.

Steve watched as Linx balled up his fist and dropped his head in frustration. "Does she always go by herself?" he asked.

With his eyes closed, Linx whispered, "Not now, mate." He turned to face Steve. "I do this every day. I watch her walk out that door and put her life into the hands of someone or something else. It's completely beyond my control. She doesn't want the help. I occasionally go with her as field support but that's it. She would rather fight on her own. I don't know why she does that, mate, and to be honest I probably don't want to know. But don't come in here pretending like you give a damn." He stood up straighter. "I've met plenty of guys like you before and the same thing happens." He looked around the room. "Don't see any here. Guess you all just disappear." He spread his arms wide and took a step back. "It's because you don't belong here. This isn't your world, mate. You can't handle it. There's more to this than you realize and guys like you don't last." He turned his back on Steve.

"I don't think that's your decision, man. Whether or not you want me around…" he paused. "Don't care. Do you make all her life choices for her? Does she ask your opinion on everything? Doubtful. And it's none of your business why I'm still here. Why can't you let her tell me herself that she doesn't want me around or are you afraid that's not the case? Are you scared she actually wants me here? That maybe you're just not enough man for her?"

Linx took a deep breath and closed his eyes. "Don't do it, mate," he said quietly.

"You've tried, haven't you? You've tried and she shot you down!" Steve teased.

"Let it go," Linx answered flatly.

"That's it! She shot you down and now you force everyone else away from her to keep her from being happy because if you can't have her…" Steve chuckled. "You'll make sure nobody else does."

Linx spun around and swung heavily. His fist connected with Steve's jaw. There was a loud crack and Steve stumbled back. "You don't get to speak about her!" Linx yelled. "You haven't earned that!"

Steve touched his jaw and smiled. "She's not here to stop me now," he growled. "You're all alone." He stared at Linx. "You don't deserve her. You're weak."

Linx leapt at Steve and knocked him to the ground. He pulled back and pounded into Steve's face twice before he was knocked to the side. His body hit the floor with a thump and a grunt.

Steve crawled over and slammed a fist into Linx's chest. Linx curled in on himself and coughed. He growled and kicked Steve in the face. Steve twisted and flew backwards. He landed with a thud. Spit and blood dribbled from his lips as he pulled himself to his knees. He fell forward again. "Kick a man while he's down? Kind of weak," Steve grumbled. He flipped himself over and eyed Linx.

"Not weak, mate. I take advantage of the situation," Linx responded. He motioned for Steve to get up. "Not giving up are you?"

"Not a chance," Steve said. He kicked Linx in the leg with a grunt and scooted backwards. He pulled himself up and laughed. "Time to fight dirty."

Haydeez brushed her fingertips over the charms on her necklace, each a symbol of someone else's religion. Each powerful to a believer, nothing to others. While she did not believe in one specific religion, she believed in the beliefs of others, and that gave each of those charms strength. She kept her eyes forward on the road. "I can beat myself up later. Now, I need to stop this," she whispered to herself.

The bridge was empty as she headed across the bay. Only emergency vehicles were allowed to cross but she had flashed one of her "badges" to the cops at the barricade. The officer had radioed to the other side that one vehicle was on the way across and then waved her forward.

She steadied her breathing and concentrated on her heartbeat. At the other side, the barricade shifted and the officers motioned for her to go. She thanked them with a nod and moved directly towards the fires. The barrier closed quickly behind her. In spite of everything, they stood at their post. She felt bad that she had to deceive them but knew that, if they knew what she was about to do, they would understand why she did.

The destruction seemed to begin down one main street and then branch off into secondary damage from there. She pulled off into a small parking area and turned off the rental. She glanced at her phone for a moment but there was still no service. With a sigh, she grabbed her bag and stuffed her phone into a pocket. "Show time," she mumbled.

The moment her door opened, the smoke accosted her. She took small breaths at first to acclimate herself. Burnt rubber, burnt buildings, and burnt flesh filled her nostrils. She closed her eyes, took a deep breath, and let it all flow over her for a few seconds. Her body accepted the smells, the heat, the pressure, and she exhaled. "Alright. Where are you?" she said aloud.

She walked between buildings to the main road. Her eyes began to water. She was not sure if it was from the smoke or what she saw, but it did not matter. The result was still the same. A tear trickled down her cheek.

Dead bodies dotted the road and sidewalks. Broken glass sparkled everywhere as it reflected the flames that raged all around. Cars sat open and abandoned in the middle of the street. Nobody was alive here. Nobody saw her stand there with her eyes wide as her brain tried to process everything. Small dead eyes looked up from the lifeless lumps of flesh to the night sky as if to beg for help.

She could not allow her emotions to take control. The entire area was decimated, so many had lost their lives, and she did not know where the Chimera was, but many more would die if she lost her focus. She let out a slow and steady breath. "I'm coming for you," she said. "And it's going to hurt."

As she moved through the streets, she took stock of her surroundings. Everything looked like pain and destruction but hidden within were little differences. An orange ball cap was in the center of the road. Three red cars were parked all in a row. She had to mark her path to be able to find her way back. Her steps were careful and swift as she followed the chaos toward the docks.

• • •

Linx stared blankly at the screen for what seemed like hours. He tried to call Haydeez on the cell several times. Inside, he knew the signal was lost but a part of him hoped that it would come back.

He watched the news coverage of the disaster. All the anchors regurgitated the same information over and over. Nobody had anything new and nobody had footage of the city.

At first, Linx attributed the outage to one of his little pulse bombs. But then he started to get concerned when her cell did not come back up. Five minutes passed, ten minutes passed, and no call came. Linx began to pace.

"So, how long do we sit here and wait before we panic?" Steve asked sarcastically. "I mean, I'm new to all of this. Is there a protocol we have to follow or do we just start flipping out at random? I'd like to make sure that I stick to the rules."

Linx stopped and turned. He shot a glare at Steve that could back off a bear. "Do you really want to go again, mate? I get that you're trying to be funny but it's not working."

Steve threw up his hands and said, "Relax. I'm not interested in another round. Just trying to lighten the mood." He sat on the couch and heaved a sigh. "What exactly are we supposed to do while we wait?" He leaned back and propped his feet up on the table. "I'm more of a doer, not a waiter."

Linx shook his head. "Yeah, looks like you have a tough time waiting." He pointed at Steve's face. "By the way, you've got a bit of something right there."

"Where?" Steve asked as he touched his face.

Linx chuckled. "Everywhere, mate." He tossed a napkin at Steve. "I don't know how you can't feel that."

Steve picked up the napkin and began to wipe his face. He winced as the napkin went over a gash on his cheek. "Found one," he laughed. "Did you scratch me like a cat or something?"

"Don't be such a baby. It won't even scar," Linx answered. "It's not like you got gored by a bull or something."

"It's a good thing I didn't," Steve chuckled. "One of those horns could tear my face off easy."

Linx froze. "Horn," he whispered. "The horn." He dropped in front of a laptop and began the click and type feverishly. "Please let it work," he mumbled. "It has to work. There's no other option. It has to work." He found the program he wanted and clicked a few more times. "Here we go," he whispered.

• • •

Haydeez stepped over bodies and around the charred remains of vehicles. The smoke was thick. She tried to take fewer breaths to avoid inhaling too much but there was no use. Everything was on fire and the odor was unbearable.

She looked around and tried to figure out which way to go. Her fingers brushed over her pocket as she fought the desire to pull out her phone. She knew there was not any service. Every piece of electronic equipment she had did not work the closer she came to the harbor. With everything that had happened, her brain tried to make sense of it all. Unfortunately for her, nothing made sense.

The path of devastation took her to a road that lead straight into the harbor. Her eyes followed the street. There were people on the ground, the same as every other street she had already been down. It looked as if they had tried to run and ended up hit from behind by a blast of fire. She started to walk through the minefield of bodies when she stopped. One of the bodies twitched. Haydeez ran up to it and turned it over to find the face of a woman, half burned off.

The woman wept. "Please, leave me alone." Her voice was hoarse and wet at the same time. "Let me die."

Haydeez wipes tears and bits of gravel from the woman's cheek. "I'm so sorry," she whispered. "I'm sorry I didn't get here sooner."

The woman coughed and blood dribbled from her lips. "Let me die. It hurts so much."

"Where did it go?" Haydeez asked as a lump formed in her throat. "I'm going to stop it. I'm going to kill it," she added, a slight twinge in her words.

With a shaky hand, the woman lifted her fingers and pointed straight down the road. "Said volcano burn," the woman tried to speak. Her voice came out in gurgles. Tears streamed down in the charred flesh on her cheek. Her body went into spasms and blood sputtered from her lips.

Haydeez held on to the woman unto the last spasm. She felt the unfortunate soul die in her arms. A shudder shook her own body. She held the woman for another moment, afraid of what she would do if she let go. After what seemed like an eternity, she laid the woman gently on the ground and closed her eyes.

Before the tears could fall, Haydeez moved her hand to cover her eyes, but she stopped. Fresh blood covered her fingertips and ran down her fingers into her palm. Her eyes lingered on the still-warm liquid. She looked down at the body of a woman she had never met, a woman who quietly begged for death. "I'm so sorry," she whispered again and turned her gaze down the street where the woman tried to point. "I'm coming."

She wiped the blood off her fingers onto the ground and stood. The arrow wiggled around in the quiver. The weight of it was a comfort on her shoulders. She reached back to feel the cold iron and moved swiftly down the road. Her feet picked up speed as she leapt over bodies and climbed onto cars. She ran, fueled by anger. There was so much anger. She was angry with Pandora for releasing the Chimera. She was angry at the Chimera for everything it had done and everything it is going to do. She was angry at the air traffic control for not being able to land sooner. A few minutes earlier would have made a difference. Then there was the anger at herself because she did not get here fast enough. She could have saved that woman and all these other innocent lives if she had just moved faster.

The sounds of screams filled her ears and she knew she was close. She raced down the road and skidded to a halt. The screams were close. She went down the side road and jumped up to grab the fire escape. Her weight barely pulled it down before she began to climb up. She moved so quickly and quietly that the steps gave no more than the occasional squeak.

The roof grew closer as she skipped steps and pulled herself along. She flung her legs over the edge of the roof and ran to the other side. As she leaned over, she let out a gasp.

On the ground beneath her stood the Chimera in all its glory. It stood a good two feet taller than her with a tail that made it twice as long. The snake head swayed back and forth. It snapped at a body on the ground that still moved. An eerily human laugh escaped the fanged jaws of the snake. It clamped down on the person's leg and began to happily drag the person back towards itself.

"It's good to see you join in the destruction, dear. We must work together to succeed," the Chimera said. It turned and reached for the snake.

The snake head dropped the person's leg and slithered up to the lion's head. It pressed against the mane and flicked its tongue against the lion's cheek lovingly. "Fighting gets us nowhere, my love. We are a family and we look out for each other," the snake hissed.

Haydeez sat down and leaned against the guard wall on the roof. "This is not what I expected," she mumbled to herself. "Not sure how to keep the snake out of the way so I can get the arrow down the lion's throat." She sighed. "This should be fun." She rubbed her hands over her face and felt bits of gravel from when she brushed off the woman's face. She rolled the gravel between her fingertips for a moment. "I said I was coming and here I am," she whispered. "I have to do this now." She pulled herself above the wall again. "Show me something to help me get an idea of how to get this arrow in your mouth, big guy."

But there was nothing. Haydeez had no idea how to do it. Of course she had fired arrows before but the targets were not aware and able to see it coming from any direction. Not to mention she had to get the arrow down his throat in one shot. She had to account for so many variables and possibilities that she began to doubt herself. There was only one arrow. What would happen if it missed the mark?

Haydeez slid down with her back to the wall again. She sat pressed against the barrier. It was difficult to hide in the shadows when there were none. Fires blazed up and down the street like a massive bonfire on the beach.

She slowed her breathing and closed her eyes. *One shot,* she thought to herself. *How am I supposed to do this?* She rolled her shoulders and let out a long slow breath. Her nerves were on end as she tried to calm herself.

A voice quietly crackled. "I don't know if you can even hear me, love, but I know you can do this. I'm still here."

Her eyes shot open. "Linx?" she whispered. "I can barely hear you." She crawled to the other side of the roof. "How am I hearing you right now?"

"Haydeez! Bloody hell! Finally! The Chimera is trashing cell signals somehow. I think it's got something to do with the weird weather stuff. I reprogrammed everything to work like a walkie," Linx answered quickly. "No video, just audio. But at least I know you're alive." He sighed.

Haydeez scoffed. "Like a little fire-breathing, three-headed weird monster thing could stop me," she said with a chuckle. "You can't get rid of me that easily. Besides, you're not strong enough to use my bow to kill this thing."

"Ha, ha, you're just too funny, love. I'm going to stay here with you until it's done. Or until I lose the connection," Linx said.

"Wouldn't have it any other way," Haydeez said with a smile. "Wait, where is the mic?" she asked. "I didn't put on anything extra before I left."

Linx chuckled. "Check your charms, love. I bet you didn't even notice the odd one mixed in with all the others."

Haydeez touched the necklace. Her fingers brushed over all the familiar shapes. She stopped on the new one. "A unicorn?" she asked as she traced the sparkling horn with her fingertip. "Why a unicorn?"

Linx blushed as he cleared his throat. "Not important. Just glad it works." He glanced at Steve. "I can shut it off when you're not on a job so you don't have to worry about me spying on you or anything. I just didn't want you to be alone out there," he added.

"Thank, Linx," Haydeez said. She pressed the charm against her collar bone where it sat and took a deep breath. "Ok, time to skin a lion." She let out the breath slowly.

•

Steve dabbed at another open wound, this time on his lip. He shook his head. "So, you can't even tell her, man?" he asked.

Linx muted his microphone on his end. "No, mate. Not happening," he answered. "It's not important enough right now."

Steve laughed. "When is it ever going to be important enough? I've been around for, what, a few weeks? She knows exactly how I feel and where I want this go. You've lived with her for years and nothing? I'd say I'll fight you for her but I think we've already covered that," he said as he gestured to the floor behind himself. He chuckled. "At least I don't have to worry about you trying to step in. You're too scared to say anything to her."

Linx waved him off. "Go do something, mate. I can't concentrate while you're talking." He turned his back to Steve.

Steve smiled and went back to his cuts and bruises. Now that the anger at each other had been released, they could focus on Haydeez and how she would survive this.

• • •

Haydeez felt a wave of relief flood her entire body. She was not alone anymore. Nobody was here with her, she had no back-up, but she was not alone. She had psyched herself out because she was afraid to fail and nobody would even know she was here.

"I'm on a roof. Steve's contact was right. It looks like that Stavros guy put his family into the Chimera. They're enjoying this. It's like some kind of demented family outing," Haydeez whispered. "Oh, and he said something about a volcano. I don't know exactly what he said because I wasn't there. That little bit of info was told to me by a lady that died in my arms." She swallowed hard. The lump refused to go away as her eyes teared up again.

Linx sat with his mouth open. "Um, let me see if I can find out anything about a volcano in that area," he said quickly. The keyboard clicked as both Linx and Steve scanned the screen.

"Oh, that doesn't look good," Steve chimed in.

"No, mate, it's not," Linx responded. "So, I think he might be trying to wake up a dormant volcano, love. He's going to try to erupt a volcano right off the coast of New England. Not only is that going to spray lava all over but the explosion will cause a massive wave that could wipe out Massachusetts easily. If he does that, you will die. You're right on the front lines." He glanced at Steve.

Steve motioned for Linx to say something. Linx shook his head and furrowed his brow. Steve rolled his eyes and said, "So basically, kill him first."

"Yup, basically," Haydeez whispered. "Easy enough." She crawled back to the other side of the roof and poked her head over the top.

The Chimera was still on the street. Even with his back to her, she still had no advantage. Where the lion's face was pointed one way, the snake looked the other. She would have to take out the snake before she could get to the lion's head. She pulled out an iron dagger and ran her fingers over the markings. "Should work," she mumbled as she watched the creature on the ground. "She said just the lion's body is impenetrable, right? So, the snake part should be vulnerable." She adjusted the dagger in her grip. She kept her gaze on the Chimera. "This whole thing will be quick. Ok, Linx, I have to take my shot. I'm going to jump off the building and take off the snake's head and then get this arrow in the lion's mouth. Easy enough, right? Yea, easy," she said.

Linx cleared his throat. "You're going to jump off a what? Why are you doing that? You don't need to jump off a building," Linx said nervously.

Haydeez scoffed. "Oh please. I fell down the inside of a tower just a couple months ago. Jumping off a five story building is no big deal," she whispered.

The building began to vibrate.

"Ok, no time to argue." Haydeez gripped the wall. "Stuff is happening. Building is shaking," she said as she stood up. "No time like the present," she added and jumped over the wall.

Linx heard the rumble on his end and yelled, "Bloody hell! Wait! Haydeez!" He gripped the edge of the table.

"Third floor has a really sturdy window box," Haydeez said casually. "I'm right above them."

Linx sighed heavily. "Don't do that again. At least now you're closer to the ground." He had to force his fingers to unclench from the table. His muscles tightened again as he heard Haydeez say, "Three, two, one."

Haydeez jumped from the window box on the third floor, dagger in hand. Her body fell straight down and onto the Chimera's back. She stabbed the snake and ripped its flesh open in one swift move. The symbols lit up and began to burn a deep purple. The snake wriggled and tried to twist around but it could not gain enough control to turn its body. The Chimera reached back with a massive clawed hand in a feeble attempt to remove Haydeez but she had already jumped off.

With her free hand she reached out for the snake and pulled it to the ground. Blood and fluids gushed out. The snake shrieked in pain. "Stop her!" she hissed.

The Chimera spun its immense body to address this new pest but moved too quickly. As he turned, Haydeez tightened her grip and ripped the rest of the flesh. The snake screamed in agony. She tossed the snake to the ground and faced the lion's head.

All four eyes looked down on her. Then, two of the eyes turned toward the snake as it wiggled on the street. Those two eyes began to brim with tears. "Calm yourself, son," the Chimera roared. "As long as we are still alive we can reattach her and she will be one with us again. She will be fine, son." All four eyes burned with anger and were once again turned to Haydeez.

"As long as you're alive you can reattach her? Interesting," Haydeez said. "Not to worry. You'll all be reunited soon enough." She planted her feet firmly on the ground and tightened her grip on the dagger.

The Chimera laughed. "That useless relic will do nothing to us. We are strong. You can break us apart, piece by piece but we will not die," he said. His voice had an odd echo, like someone had repeated everything he said.

"Are you ready to take that chance?" she asked with a smirk. She flicked the dagger back and forth between her fingers. "Tick tock. What's it going to be, kitty? Want to test your theory?" She cocked her head to the side and smiled.

Haydeez glanced around the street as a low rumble started. As it grew, she expected buildings to crumble and cracks to open in the street. But everything remained calm. Nothing shook, nothing broke, and yet the rumble grew.

Just as it developed into a deafening peak, she turned back to the Chimera who stood calmly with a hideous smile on its jaws. Fangs the size of a grown man's finger protruded from its gums. He chuckled. "We believe that we are safe. We are willing to take the supposed 'risk' as you put it. How safe do you feel?" he asked.

Chapter 33

Before Haydeez could answer, the Chimera let out a roar that shattered the windows above her head. Glass rained down around her in razor sharp chunks. She ran to avoid the shards.

"What's going on, Haydeez?" Linx shouted. "What's all that noise?"

"Oh, just glass shattering and falling on me," she answered in a huff. "Oops," she said as her foot slipped slightly. "Didn't expect that."

Another rumble vibrated the air around her. Haydeez turned around to see the Chimera open its massive jaws.

"Aw, crap," she mumbled as she turned back around and raced across the road. A blinding flame shot from the Chimera's mouth. The fire traveled on the waves of a bellow that echoed between the buildings.

She slid behind two cars that had previously collided on the side of the road. "I don't think he likes me at all. And I thought we were going to be the best of friends forever," she said to Linx. Something sizzled behind her head. "What is that sound?" she asked herself. When she poked her head up over the cars, there were almost no vehicles left.

The metal was scorched and melted into a twisted junk yard sculpture. A fire blazed in the middle of it all like a hearth on a winter night. "This is not going to end well," Haydeez muttered. She looked down and eyed the exposed fuel tank and added, "Oh, come on," she yelled as she bolted to her feet and took off at a sprint. The fire tore through the fuel tank as Haydeez ran. Without so much as a look over her shoulder, she raced past debris to get out of the blast range.

An explosion rocked the buildings and molten shards of car pieces sprayed out in all directions. Heat and fire flew out from the center. The Chimera let out a laugh that thundered down the street.

"What's happening?" Linx shouted. "Are you alright?"

"Just a minute please," Haydeez yelled breathlessly. "Little busy." She scanned the area for a higher perch. Ahead and to the left was a short building with an awning. As she came close, her feet came off the ground and she grabbed the awning. She pulled her body up and leapt up to the roof. "That was a couple of cars exploding behind me, the same cars I had just hid behind. That thing just spewed some kind of weird fire that can burn anything. Not to mention it's super-hot, so everything melts. Now that we're all caught up, I'm trying to make a tactical retreat here." She reached for her bow and let out a long sigh. "Ok, here we go." She closed her eyes and just felt the weight of the bow for a moment. "Time to stop playing," she mumbled to herself.

Haydeez tested the tension in her bow string and pulled out the iron arrow. The weight was vastly different than the usual arrows in her quiver. "This is going to work, right? It has to work. It'll work," she said to herself. "Just aim and shoot. Same as always. It's just another arrow and that mouth is just another target... full of fire... that shoots out at me. Easy enough."

"Relax, love. You can do this," Linx said calmly. "I can't see you but in my head I can see you getting ready. You're making sure your hair is back and out of your face, and your jacket isn't too tight. My guess is that you've already found the best spot to take the shot. You're ready."

Haydeez released a long steady breath. "I got this," she said.

Linx sat on the other end with his eyes glued to a screen. The only thing it showed him was that the connection was still active. Steve stood at his side, fingers clenched into fists. They both held their breath as they waited to hear something on the other side.

The vibrations had stopped. The roars were quieted. Not even the crackle of a fire could be heard. Linx and Steve could only hear the soft whisper of her slow, steady breath.

●　　●　　●

Haydeez stood up, bow in hand. She nocked the iron arrow and walked to the edge of the roof. The Chimera stood in the middle of the road.

"Come out, puny human," the Chimera bellowed. "You can't possibly believe that you have a chance to stop us. Our enemies will fear us, bow down before us. We're no longer just a man, someone trying to grow his business, anymore. We're a god, taking control, destroying those who oppose us," it said as it walked slowly up the street. "Nobody is stronger than us. Nobody will stop us! We are indestructible!" The Chimera laughed.

"That was your first mistake. You never say that," she mumbled and shook her head. "I believe we haven't been properly introduced," Haydeez said loudly as she swung her leg over the side of the roof. "My name is Haydeez." She pulled back on the bow string and aimed. "But you can call me 'Nobody'. I'll be killing you today," she added with a smirk.

The Chimera turned to face Haydeez. It smiled. "We shall see, human." As it sucked in air, the ground vibrated again. A roar flew from its jaws. More windows shattered, the buildings shook, but Haydeez held her position. A white hot flame spewed from the lion's mouth straight towards her. At the same time, she let the arrow fly right into the center of the blaze. As soon as it was on its way, she threw herself backwards onto the roof to avoid the fire. The flames grazed the tip of her moccasin enough to catch it on fire. She quickly pulled it off and began to bang out the flame on the roof. "No! These are my favorite!" she yelled.

The only response she received was a loud gurgle and muffled scream.

She pulled herself up over the edge and looked down at the ground. A smile spread across her lips. "I did it. I totally freaking did it! Linx, I got him!" She laughed.

The Chimera grabbed at the end of the arrow and tried to pull it out. It used all its strength as it gagged on the melted iron but it was too late. The arrow had melted in the immense heat and coated the creature's throat. It began to suffocate.

Haydeez could see the creature heave as it tried to spew another wave of fire. One set of eyes looked up to her as if to plead for help. She forced herself to maintain her gaze with what she believed was the child's eyes as she shook her head. There was no person left. This was a creature of destruction and it had to be stopped. "You're not a child anymore. You're a monster," she whispered.

Silence spread through the streets as the Chimera dropped to the ground and writhed in agony. "I didn't realize it took so long to suffocate someone," she whispered. Her voice boomed in the silence.

Something moved in the corner of her eye. She snapped her head to the right. On the ground, she saw someone with the snake cradled in her arms. The person stroked the snake calmly.

"Who the hell is that?" Haydeez asked.

"What's going on now? Is someone else there?" Linx asked.

"Looks that way, she said as she swung her leg over the side of the building. "Let's go find out." She slid down onto the awning and dropped to the ground. Bow still in hand, she began to walk towards the figure.

As she got closer, she could see that a woman held the snake's body. The woman wore next to nothing, yet she showed no signs of the cold that beat down the edges of the fires. She stroked the snake's body and whispered a soft song. "She's dying and she doesn't even realize it," the woman said quietly.

Haydeez stood with her brow furrowed. "You're a siren," she said matter-of-factly. "Why are you here?"

The siren smiled down at the creature as it slipped peacefully into oblivion. "I am here to help my brother, however you have destroyed him. His life is slowly escaping his body as we speak." Her words sounded as if she could not care whether he lived or died. She merely stated a fact. "They will be at peace soon enough." She looked up at Haydeez and smiled.

"Did she say siren?" Steve asked.

"There's a siren there? Haydeez, don't let her touch you! You can fight her voice, but if she touches you," he paused. "Just don't let her near you."

Haydeez shook her head. "If he's dying, she's dying, you can't help them anymore. Why are you still here?" she asked.

The siren's song stopped. "They have passed." She lifted her gaze to meet Haydeez. "I'm here to help you, sister." Her hand rose. "Come. There is much for us to do together."

Haydeez took a step backwards. "Not a chance. I hear it's bad to touch you and I'm not about to become some mindless follower."

"Uh, Haydeez. Do you have those little bombs with you?" Linx asked nervously.

With her eyes fixed on the siren, she said, "Yeah, of course. Why?"

Linx stared at the screen. "Because the static is clearing. Set it off now!"

Chapter 34

"You need to kill it and get out of there. That bomb won't last forever, love. You don't need people recognizing you," Linx said. He quickly added, "What's that noise?"

The siren's song began to trickle through the speakers. Linx shook his head violently. He groaned. "I can't stay on, love. It's coming through. The song is coming through. You've got this. She's no match for you," he grunted. With one hand pressed against his head, he slammed his other hand on the keyboard and dropped the connection. "I'm sorry," he whispered.

Linx took a deep breath and turned around. "You alright, mate?" he asked. He paused as his gaze stopped on Steve who stood completely still except the steady rise and fall of his chest. His eyes were wide and blank, pupils dilated.

"Hey, Steve," Linx said as he snapped his fingers in front of Steve's face. "Stop playing games, mate. This isn't funny. That thing isn't even here." He grabbed Steve by the shoulders and shook him.

Steve lifted his arms and shoved Linx backwards in one swift movement. Steve's eyes never moved and the rest of his body remained rigid.

"You can't even hear that thing anymore. Knock it off," Linx yelled. He walked back up to Steve and pushed him in the chest. "Enough!"

Steve swiped at Linx to push him to the side. Linx side-stepped and used the momentum of Steve's swing to throw him off-balance. As Linx pushed Steve further to the left, Steve's body fell to the floor. Linx kneeled on his back.

With a grunt, Linx said, "I don't want to have to hurt you, but I will snap your neck. Now knock it off! Get it out of your head! It's not here. It has no control over you anymore." He grunted again and put his other knee on Steve's arm. "I'm not moving until you're you again, mate."

• • •

"We could be amazing together, sister. You can hear my song, yet it doesn't enthrall you," the siren cooed. "Aunt Pandora would appreciate more females to join us. With all of us together, nothing would stand in our way." The creature smiled.

Haydeez shook her head. "Nope. I think I'll pass. As aggravating as men are, I think I still want to keep them around."

The siren laughed. "They are quite amusing, aren't they? I would love to keep some around as toys, but Aunt Pandora insists that we destroy all of them. Pity. I could see many uses for them and of course I could keep them content to do whatever I want." She took a step towards Haydeez. "I truly believed you would be different. I thought you would join us. I had hoped you would take up the side of your sisters. After all, you are like me. I'm not sure what you are yet but I can see that you are definitely one of us."

Haydeez looked down at herself and then back at the siren. "Um, yeah I'm a female. Not sure what you're talking about but it doesn't really matter. I'm kind of on the clock here. So, let's get this over with so I can go home. I'm kind of alone here and I don't do well with lonely." She strapped the bow to her back and pulled the dagger back out. "Only one of us is walking away and I'm pretty sure you can guess who that's going to be." She spread out her arms and smiled. "Ready to die?"

The siren ran her fingers through her hair and smiled back. "I will remember you along with all the men of the world. Are you certain that you will not join us?" she asked one last time.

Haydeez rolled her eyes. She lunged at the siren and swept her hand across the siren's stomach. "Answer your question?"

With a pout on her lips, the siren stepped out of the way and grabbed at her wrist.

Don't let her touch you. Haydeez heard Linx in her head. She jerked her hand away quickly. "Not so fast, sweetheart. I have no desire to hold hands with you." She flipped the dagger in her hand. The blade sat flat against her wrist. "Not my type." As she struck out with the blade, Haydeez held her breath.

The blade caught the siren's flesh and ripped open a gash across her chest. Silver liquid spilled out and the siren gasped.

Haydeez could hear the siren's song skip like someone had bumped into a record player. "Bet that didn't feel so hot." She waved the dagger. "I guess iron hurts you guys, huh? Good to know." Her eyes drifted to the drips on the ground. "Mercury. Guess we're still learning something."

The siren gripped her wound and glared at Haydeez. Her eyes narrowed. "It does not matter what you do to me. You think you are winning but you are only aiding her more with every life you take." The siren laughed. "You speak of how you would never side with her and yet here you are, stealing another life. As her power grows, you do exactly what she wants you to do. No matter what you choose, she is victorious." She looked at her fingers and licked the mercury. "It truly is a shame, sister. We could have been great together."

Haydeez took another swipe with the dagger and the siren stood with her arms spread wide. The blade struck the creature in the neck. Silver liquid sprayed out onto the ground. Haydeez cocked her head to the side and furrowed her brow. She watched as the creature fell to the ground with a smile on her face. The metallic blood poured out all over the ground.

As the creature's body convulsed, an eerie laugh gurgled out of her mouth. Then everything stopped. The only sound was the fire that still crackled all around her.

Haydeez stood in the road, confused. "What the hell just happened?" she asked. With nobody to respond, all she could do was look around at the massacre. "Anybody? No?" She pulled out her phone. "Still no signal. Ok, I need to go." With a quick glance around, she grabbed what she could of the iron arrow and took off at a run.

Her coat flapped behind her as she raced through the deserted streets. She glanced around for the familiar objects she had mentally tagged earlier. There were the three red cars lined up in a row. The orange ball cap had not moved. Her rental was around the corner. There was still nobody around.

After she checked her phone one more time, she climbed into the driver's seat and took a deep breath. She tried to process everything the siren had said. Anger, frustration, confusion, and a twinge of fear bubbled up to the surface and tears flowed down her cheeks. She screamed. "I don't know what to do! What am I supposed to do?" she asked over and over. With her hands over her face, she screamed again.

The sound of her scream was interrupted by her ringtone. She quickly sniffled and wiped the tears away. "Linx! They're gone! I killed them all," she said before he could even say hello.

"I had a feeling," he answered. "One minute I've got my knee in Steve's back. The next he's yelling at me to get off. Once that thing died, it must've broken the hold over him. And I would just like to point out that he went under pretty quick. I mean, fast." He chuckled.

In the background, Haydeez could hear Steve say, "Wow, dude. That's the first thing you say. I thought we had worked everything out, you know, friends and all. I see how it is."

Haydeez smiled. "I need to get out of here as quickly as possible. I don't need anyone to see me out here. Where are the news crews?"

Chapter 35

"I'm through," Haydeez said as she pulled away from the bridge. The bay grew smaller in her rear view mirror. "Time to get out of here. The quakes have stopped at least. I think it's safe to say that the volcano didn't get the chance to erupt." She sighed.

"You did everything you could. Not everyone can say they saved the world, right?" Linx joked. "Have you called the pilot? Do you know where you're meeting him yet?" he asked.

Haydeez tapped the location into her GPS and said, "Yup, on my way right now. I'll let you know when we're in the air. Honestly, I just want to sleep in my own bed tonight. I can't believe how much damage he caused. It was devastating to see in person. I seriously feel guilty leaving right now. All those people are dead and I'm just driving away because my job is done. Who does that?"

Linx sighed. "I'm not going to say you're wrong for leaving, but what do you think you're going to do for them? Not to sound cruel but what more can you do? You hunt and kill things, not bury the dead. Your job is to stop the threat and make sure nobody else gets hurt. There are so many people right now that need help but your skills are not what they need. The way to help people is to stop Pandora. If you don't, everyone dies. Then it won't matter. You wouldn't want a paramedic going after her, right?" He paused. "Once she's stopped, we can all take a break. It's not like threats like this come up all the time. Don't worry, love. This will end," he added with a tired attempt at optimism.

"I'll call you when we're in the air," Haydeez repeated. "It'll be a couple hours. He had to take the plane south." She turned and headed towards the interstate. "There's a little airstrip south of the city but with all the damage, traffic is slow. I wonder how far in they felt the shaking? I thought the building was going to collapse under me."

"Do you want me to stay on with you?" Linx asked. "You sound like you don't want to be alone. You don't even have to talk. Just keep me on the line."

With a heavy sigh, she just said, "Thank you."

She merged her rental onto the interstate. All the traffic seemed to be on the opposite side of the road. Lights flashed as emergency vehicles raced north past her. She counted them as they sped away. "There are more fire trucks, EMTs, and cops on this road than regular cars," she mumbled.

"Lots of people coming to help," Linx said quietly.

Haydeez sniffled. "Good."

She drove in silence for a few more minutes. The sirens began to lessen. Her eyes moved back and forth on either side of the road. "Starting to get empty," she said. She began to make her way around a large curve. Her eyes stopped on something off to the right. With her foot on the brake, she drifted off to the shoulder. "What the hell?" she said.

"What now?" Linx asked.

"She's here. I can see her watching me from a hill off the road. I need to stop."

• • •

"Well hello, child. I was not certain if you would see me from that large road. I am content that you did not miss me," Pandora said with a smile. She stood bathed in moonlight. There were not many trees in the area of the park that she had chosen.

Haydeez moved around her vehicle and toward Pandora. "What happened to you?" she asked.

An eerie smile spread across Pandora's lips. "I have aged greatly this night. Not only did you take the life of the Chimera I released, which of course was three creatures all in one, but you also took the life of a siren. Both of them were mine as you know. They were full of incredible power and helped me build up what I need to complete my task." She chuckled. "Even one such as myself requires a small amount of assistance."

"Ok, so I know you take their essence but what I didn't know is that it made you get older," Haydeez said. "I don't see how that helps you at all."

Pandora chuckled again. "Simple Haydeez. How do you not see? The child I was before could not handle the upcoming undertaking. It could not hold all the power that I needed to perform the calling ritual that brings the first man and woman born of this earth together. It requires an adult form. While I appreciate the irony of taking over a child called Eve when I am trying to destroy the first man and woman, her body was not ready. I had to help it along to make it into the vessel that I required." She spread her arms out and looked at them. "As you can see, it is nearing the final stages. Soon, this body will be able to hold enough power to perform the final mission. There is truly nothing that you will be able to do to prevent me from ending man." Pandora smiled. "The beginning of the end is already upon us. There is much sadness across the world this night. When I caused the egg to summon those two unfortunate souls, it caused a chain reaction that left many families in tears. If they knew what was looming in their futures, this minor trouble would be the least of their insignificant worries. Fortunately, the egg is not only bringing me the two souls I need to destroy man, but it also started the process for me. Unfortunately, it depleted a great deal of my energy. This is why I needed you to take care of those," she paused as she searched for the word. "Useless... yes useless, but powerful creatures. I needed the boost to rebuild and grow."

Haydeez cocked an eyebrow and chuckled. "I just have one question, and it's an easy one so there shouldn't be too much thought involved. Are you going to continue to monologue? I mean, right now it's like 'cheesy spy movie villain' bad but hey, who am I to stop you? I just wanted to know if you're going to continue. Don't get me wrong. I'd love to know your whole plan and how you intend to do it. It's always good to be prepared and stuff."

Pandora's eyes opened wide for a moment and her brow furrowed. She regained her composure and answered. "I am not sure what it is that you are referring to, however, it will not harm my plans to share them with you. Unfortunately for you, there is no way for you to stop me. Therefore, whether you know or not will be of no consequence."

"Nice to see I could catch you off guard. Show's me that there's still a chance to beat you," Haydeez said. "And I will."

"When I am finished, there will be nothing left for you to save. Man will be gone. All that will be left are creatures like those I have released, and me. Perhaps when everything is gone, you will see why your crusade has been an exercise in futility. Eventually you will see why it would have been simpler to just join me, child." Pandora chuckled again. "Eve," she mumbled.

Haydeez furrowed her brow this time. "What? So wait, you're only destroying men? Now I'm really lost. I thought you were supposed to destroy humans, you know, mankind, and now you're telling me that I'll still be alive. Do you even know what you're doing? It sounds like you're just making it all up as you go along. Aren't you supposed to follow some kind of plan or rules or something?" Haydeez asked.

Pandora laughed. "You still do not understand, child. When the world ends and we are all that remains, perhaps you will comprehend what has happened. There is something different inside you and when man reaches his demise, maybe you will finally see, we will all finally see what is hidden inside of you. There is something there. But your secret is shrouded. I cannot see what is inside."

Haydeez shook her head. "What the hell are you talking about? You're not making any sense!" she yelled. "Why does everyone always have to talk in riddles? Why can't you just say what you mean and be done with it?"

Pandora laughed again. "Life is never as easy as one would hope it to be, child. When my father created me, he knew I would be needed to restart the world. Humans cannot be trusted to take care of the gifts they have. My father knew that from the start. That is why he gave me the doorway to oblivion," she said as she looked down at the golden disk around her neck. "The creatures never truly die, if they can make it back here. Their essence remains inside where I can hold them until I have need of their devastating capabilities."

Haydeez just watched Pandora. The dial pulsed quietly with a dim golden glow. Then she asked, "What about the ones I kill?"

Pandora smiled. "They become me. Without them, I cannot grow. Some must be sacrificed for the... greater good," she answered with her arms spread wide. "What greater good can there be beyond fulfilling your sole purpose in life? After so many years waiting, I will finally make my father proud. I will become everything that he ever wanted for me and so much more. When I was created, there were so few humans. While it is true that I was meant to destroy man, the extinction of a species with a few thousand is nothing. However, the total annihilation of billions across an entire planet is going to be spectacular!" Her eyes grew wide. "The pure bliss will be more than I ever imagined."

"Why does he want to kill humans?" Haydeez asked.

Pandora laughed. "You have never heard of my story?" she asked. "How disappointing. No matter. Humans have plagued my father since they came into existence. So many believed that I was the first human, but I am immortal. I was made of the gods, by the gods. My children usher in the renewal, generation after generation. They have kept your precious humans alive, but not for long. Once I've broken the cycle, humans will cease to be."

"I really had hoped that part was wrong. Someone who not only wants to destroy the world but is willing to kill her own children to do it? That's a whole other level of evil. How can you even think that's ok?" Haydeez asked.

"It is my purpose, my sole reason for being," Pandora answered matter-of-factly. "The stories all claim that I was frightened when I opened the jar and released all the evil. What they failed to remember is that I was given gifts by the gods. I was given beauty and immortality but they also bestowed the gifts of deceit and cunning. I knew what would be released. I wanted to set it all free. I merely pretended to be scared." She laughed. "Epimetheus believed that I was a terrified pawn when in reality I was like a General commanding an army of pure evil that traveled out across the world."

Haydeez sighed. "So, there's really no way to convince you to stop. You actually want to do this." She rubbed her hands over her eyes and groaned. "There has to be a way to stop you, and I will find it. I can't let you destroy everyone."

"You do not have a choice, child. There is not enough power within you to stop me and you cannot kill me," Pandora answered. "Your useless little humans will be gone and you are powerless to stop it."

"Wait," Haydeez said as her brow furrowed. "Zeus created you, right? But he's also the father of your children? And nobody sees anything wrong with this?" She looked around at the empty park for support. "Anybody?" she yelled.

Pandora laughed. "Your ideas of family differ greatly from those of us who are immortal. Zeus is a biological father to me as much as Hephaestus. He is a parent in the way that Athena or Aphrodite gave birth to me like a mother. They all created me and bestowed gifts upon me. In essence, they were all my parents. Does that clarify enough for you, child?" Pandora asked.

"Nope, still creepy," Haydeez answered.

Pandora shook her head. "So short-sighted, child. Try to see the events with purpose. Look to the future and the grand scheme of things instead of your small-minded vision of the world in which you live. When your world ends and you are left empty and alone, you will see. You will understand."

"Stop saying that!" Haydeez yelled. "I'm not who or what you think I am! When you kill everyone, I will die too!" She balled her fists and clenched her teeth.

Pandora smiled. "You will see, child."

Haydeez growled and let out a scream. "Stop! Enough with all these riddles and the cryptic talk. I'm not what you think I am. I don't even know what you're talking about. I'm just me, ok? Nothing special, nothing fancy. I know who I am."

"Poor thing. Left in the dark for so many years," Pandora answered. "Perhaps when everything is done, your eyes will be opened to your past. One should always know where they come from to know where they are going." She sighed. "We will see each other again soon. You will see my creatures sooner. Take heed, child. Whether you kill the creature or leave it to continue its rampage, I will gain power. You may save a few lives now but ultimately they will all die. Everyone will die. You cannot save them, child."

Before Haydeez could respond, Pandora faded from the grassy field in the middle of the park. "Oh come on!" Haydeez shouted. She looked all around the area but she knew that there was nobody near. "Seriously!" she groaned and yelled. Her phone was in her hand but she did not need to press any buttons because Linx was already there. "Did you hear all that? Please tell me you heard it and recorded it or something because I seriously have no idea what she's talking about and now I'm not just confused. I'm aggravated too."

"Got it all but I hate to tell you this. I have no clue what she's talking about either. She seems to think there's something inside you that you don't know about," Linx said. "But wouldn't you know if you're not human. I mean, you look human to me, love."

Haydeez closed the door to her rental and started the engine. "I would think so. Look, I am so sick of everyone talking in riddles. For once I would like to deal with someone who just says 'I'm going to blow up this building' or 'I'm going to rob this bank'. It would be so great to fight a straightforward bad guy for a change." She pulled back onto the highway and made her way south towards the small airfield where her plane awaited her arrival.

Linx chuckled. "Those are human bad guys and you don't deal in human stuff. The stuff you do is never just cut and dry. Supernatural evil is usually overly convoluted and complicated. And for some reason it takes a weird weapon or piece of metal nobody has ever heard of or something to do the job. That part I don't get. Why can't it just be a kitchen knife or some hedge clippers or something?"

"Because there's no fun in that," Haydeez joked. "Plus, I'd be out of a job if anyone off the street could hunt these things."

"Good point. I guess we'll just stick with the crazy weapons then," Linx said with a chuckle.

Chapter 36

Haydeez walked in her front door. She hung her coat in the closet and placed her shoes in an open cubby. "Linx!" she called out.

Linx and Steve walked into the living room. "Welcome home," Linx said.

"Could you make sure everything in my bag is alright, please?" she asked as she handed him her duffle bag.

His brow furrowed slightly in confusion for a moment. Then he nodded and took the bag down to the basement.

Haydeez motioned to the couch. "Have a seat," she said to Steve. She sat in one of the plush chairs.

Steve sat across from her and eyed her in bewilderment. "What's going on?" he asked tentatively.

She took a deep breath and sighed. "You need to go."

"Well, that's very straight-forward," Steve interrupted.

Haydeez sighed again. "It's obvious this world isn't for you. It's dangerous in a way you've never experienced before and it's not fair to put your life in danger when you don't even know what you're up against. Hell, I don't even know what we're dealing with half the time. Look," she paused. "For some reason, I was raised in this world. For some reason, I'm good at what I do. You're good at your job but this," she waived around at nothing and paused again. "This is so different. You can't just use bullets and cuffs. Sometimes, whatever you're hunting wants to eat you." She looked up at him. Their eyes locked. "At first, you were arrogant, rude, and I just wanted to put a bullet in you. Now, I hate myself for letting you in because you don't belong here. You're not weak by any definition of the word, but you're not ready. Not ready for me, not ready for what I do, not ready for my life. That's why I need you to leave. There's too much at stake right now for me to see where this could go. I want to, believe me I do, but I can't let myself lose focus and worry more about you than what I need to do. Does any of that make sense?" she asked.

Steve took a deep breath and let it out slowly. "Yea, no really, totally makes sense. I get it. I'm an outsider. I don't know what I'm doing. I have no idea how to protect myself against any of those weird creature things. Makes sense. Not to mention I'm absolutely no help when it comes to researching or figuring out how to beat them either. I really have nothing going for me. So, yup, I get it."

Haydeez sighed. "It's not a matter of whether you have anything to offer. It has nothing to do with that. I'm not always the one to figure everything out. Most of the time it's a combined effort. The problem is that I'm a target. I get hired by a lot of powerful, secretive people. The government is probably watching me right now. It's just hard to find time for much else."

"I know I'm not trained. I'm not special. There's nothing I can do," Steve replied.

"It's just not fair to either of us. You're obviously not comfortable here. I can't spare any time worrying about whether or not you're in danger. Taking you with me to Greece has shown me that. You have no idea what's actually out there. You saw that fox. That thing scared the hell out of you. And it only gets worse from there," Haydeez said as she leaned forward in her seat and reached for his hands. "The problem is that I actually like you. So, I have to push you away to make sure you stay safe."

Steve looked Haydeez in the eyes for a moment and then said, "I could learn. I already know more than I did when we first met. Look, we met under the most... inopportune situation. But that doesn't mean we can't see where this can go. Don't you think we owe it to ourselves to give it a shot?"

Haydeez sighed and dropped her head onto his hands. "I wish it was all that easy. For anyone else it probably is." She lifted her head and looked him in the eyes again. "But for me, there's just too many factors. It's not that you can't learn, or that you won't get comfortable, or even whether or not you would fit in. I'm not sure what you've shown me is really you. No matter how much I like you, I have to wonder if what I like is really you," Haydeez said. "I owe it to myself to wait until I don't have doubts. I rushed into something once because I thought it was what I was supposed to do. He said all the right things and I never thought of what was best for me. I thought he was the man that would make me feel normal in spite of my doubts. I can't do that again."

"What doubts do you have? I mean, sure, we don't know that much about each other but what are you afraid of?" Steve asked.

"To be honest, a lot of it has to do with how we met. I feel like we were introduced with a lie. Everything going forward would be built on that shaky foundation," she responded. As she sat back in her chair and released his hands, she added, "That would always be in the back of my mind. I get why you did it but it would still be there. It would take a lot for me to get past it. There will always be a part of me that questions your motives."

Steve looked down at his now empty hands and sighed. He sat quietly for several moments and just stared. "I guess there's no changing your mind then." He put his hands on his knees and pushed himself up. "I'll just see myself out," he added and walked towards the door. With his hand on the door knob, he paused. He turned around with a smirk. "I don't know when but I'll see you again. That's a promise." He moved back towards the door and closed it behind himself.

"I'm sure you will," Haydeez whispered. She stood with her eyes on the door.

"Are you alright, love?" Linx asked from the kitchen doorway.

Haydeez chuckled. "That's a loaded question. Actually, I think I'm pretty good." She turned around and playfully pushed passed Linx into the kitchen. "Could use a drink though."

Chapter 37

"Hello, i-na-bi. It is good to hear from you," Blackhawk said over the phone. "To what do I owe the pleasure today?"

Haydeez placed a mug of hot chocolate on the table and then flopped down on the couch. "Well, it looks like we're just helping her gain power. Every time I kill something, she just gets stronger. But I can't just leave whatever it is out there, roaming around." She groaned. "I hate this."

"Ah, Pandora," he chuckled. "You are not supposed to enjoy it. Besides, you will figure out what to do." The sound of a tea kettle whistle pierced the line. "You know I am here to help if you need it. You are never too experienced to admit you need a hand."

With a sigh, Haydeez said, "Yeah, yeah, yeah. I know. It's just... I should be able to handle this. I can hunt. I can fight. Why can't I figure out how to stop her?" She slid down on the couch and pulled her feet up.

"I-na-bi, you are an intelligent woman. You have the capabilities to figure it out eventually," he answered. "Besides, you have so many people working with you. There is bound to be a good idea amongst all those brains. You cannot tell me that a group of adults is not capable of formulating a plan?" he added.

Haydeez sighed. "Sometimes I don't want to be an adult. I really wish I could go back and be a kid for a while. Don't get me wrong. You've been amazing and I love you for everything you've done for me but where was my childhood?"

Linx put his hand on the kitchen door and paused. Her conversation floated over to him. For a moment, he wanted to walk away but something stopped him. It was not a desire to hear everything or be nosy. Linx heard pain in her voice. He had seen her train, fight, kill, but it was rare to see her vulnerable.

He stood out of sight and allowed Haydeez to say what she needed. It made him feel guilty but he was frozen in place.

"I didn't have friends when I was little. I had targets. I didn't play with dolls. I trained with knives. Sometimes part of me wants to be a kid again. That's probably why I act the way I do with Linx. He's been my friend for years and I can be the kid with him that I couldn't be when I actually was a kid. Having him around gives me the chance to have my childhood. It's really hard for me to be around anyone else." She sighed heavily. "I don't know. Maybe I just don't appreciate what I have or what it took to get here."

Linx looked at the floor. He turned around and sat at the kitchen table. With a heavy sigh, he rubbed his face.

"Have you told him this?" Blackhawk asked.

"Tell him he's my best friend? He already knows that. I mean, come on, he lives in my house," she answered.

Blackhawk laughed. "When you figure it out, you be sure to let him know. Now, as far as your agent friends, I found out that you have been on their radar for a while. Matter of fact, their organization is not too happy with you for snatching up Linx. From what I gather, they wanted him bad but you managed to say the right things and now they are watching you." He paused. "I guess technically that means both of you are going to be their priority for a while."

"I didn't realize they wanted him that bad. He wasn't even there for that long. And it was how many years ago? They can't still be mad about that," she said with her brow furrowed. "Hey, Linx!" she shouted. "Come here!"

Linx came into the living room a minute later. "Something wrong?" he asked.

Haydeez shook her head. "Guess who wants you?"

Color crept into his cheeks. "What?"

"D.O.G.M.A. That's why Red and Blue were following us. It's probably why they were in Greece when I found the arrow too," she answered. "Joseph says they're probably mad because I grabbed you away from them. So, now they're a bit ticked at me. I feel so popular," she added with a smirk.

Linx sat down in a chair and said, "If anyone should feel popular, it's me. Would you even have their eye if I wasn't here?" He smiled and leaned back in his seat.

"I'm pretty sure that I'll do something that will interest them at some point. Just remember, I took you away from them. So, yea, they don't like me," she responded.

Blackhawk sighed. "Does not matter who they hate more right now. You need to be careful when you are hunting. I do not want them to get in your way and end up being the reason you get hurt. You do not know how well they are trained, if they are trained."

"Not everyone can be as awesome as us," Linx said with a smile. "But he does have a point. Just imagine what could've happened if they had interfered while you were out on that boat or worse, when you were in the tower and the golem woke up. I doubt they will care who they hurt while they're trying to get what they want."

"Well, maybe we should contact them directly. Instead of waiting for them to come to me and hinder my fight with Pandora, why don't we take it to them?" Haydeez asked. "They want to be all scary and intimidating. I can show them scary."

Blackhawk paused for a moment. "I do not think that is a bad idea. They want to try to get involved, maybe they should be a part of this. They know about both of you and we know the organization is aware of the work you do. Perhaps if they were told what the world is up against, they could be convinced to fight with you or, better yet, step out of your way."

Haydeez shrugged. "Or I could just make them move. Either way it should make for an interesting conversation." She looked around for a moment. "Where did I put that card?" she asked herself.

"What card?" Linx asked.

She unzipped a side pocket on her duffel bag. "Here it is. They gave me a card to contact them. It's literally got just the phone number on it. It should say 'Creepy, weird, secret organization that's been following you'." She shook her head. "So, how about we make a call?"

"Call me back if you run into any problems, i-na-bi," Blackhawk said and hung up.

Haydeez dialed the number on the card and waited for an answer. She flipped the card over between her fingers as the line rang.

A familiar male voice answered with a slight accent. "Ms. Blackhawk. So good of you to call. I take it you would like to meet," he said matter-of-factly.

Haydeez sighed. "Yup. Let's get together. We can meet somewhere," she answered.

"Wonderful. Should we pick you up?" As he asked the question her front gate buzzer went off. There was silence for a moment and then he added, "Are you going to get that?"

With a look that rivaled an angry bear, Haydeez hung up the phone and pushed the button. "Do you camp outside my property or did you just happen to be driving by my front gate?"

Linx looked at Haydeez, his eyes wide. "Are they actually out there right now?" he asked.

She nodded. "You can wait outside until I come up there." Her fists clenched and she closed her eyes. Heat rose from her face and her cheeks flushed with anger. She let out a slow steady breath and opened her eyes. "I hate presumptuous uninvited guests. Let's go." With her coat in hand, she headed out the door with Linx right behind.

They walked up to the gate and saw Agent Blue and Agent Red on the other side. With a smile, Agent Blue said, "Glad you finally decided to talk to us, Ms. Blackhawk. Mr. Van Martin, I see you're doing well for yourself. I suppose sleeping your way into money does work."

Linx clenched his fists and moved to jump through the fence and then the Agent, but Haydeez pushed him back.

"Words like that will not get you what you want, *Agent.* I've been pleasant for our previous encounters. Do not test me," Haydeez said calmly.

Agent Blue chuckled. "Of course. So, straight to business then. You've obviously contacted us for a reason. I take it we're not permitted onto your property as you haven't even cracked the gate. So, please, the floor is yours." He motioned in front of her.

Haydeez crossed her arms. "You need to step back. You're getting into something that I'm sure is way beyond your pay grade and skill level. Just let me do my job and the world will stay safe. If you continue to get in my way, I can't promise you'll stay safe. That's not a threat. It's a fact. I can't waste my time trying to protect you and take care of this issue at the same time. So, it's your choice. Back off or take your life into your own hands."

Agent Red smiled. "And what exactly is this 'issue' as you've called it? You haven't really given us a reason to believe that you're not the problem here. How do we know that you're not the one that we should be watching?" he asked.

Haydeez laughed. "Wow, your agency really is that stupid. If you think I'm a danger then I dare you to try to stop me. Then again, if that's what you thought, you would've come after me already. So, one of two things is happening here. Either you're here because you're still pissed about me taking Linx from you, which is pretty sad. He wasn't really there for that long and he didn't have a high enough clearance to be worth much to you." She glanced at Linx and added, "No offense."

Linx shrugged with a smile. "None taken."

Haydeez turned back to the gate and continued. "Or, you have no clue what's going on and you need me to figure it out for you. Now, I'm thinking that's what's happening here and quite frankly, I don't appreciate your attitude. If you want help, then ask but don't camp outside my home or follow me around the world while I try to deal with this." She cocked her head to the side. "So, which is it? Still mad or you need my help?"

Linx stood next to her and smirked. "Yup, she's that good. Guess you can see why I left."

Agent Blue narrowed her eyes. "Cute. You're not important enough to us to follow you years after you left us, Mr. Van Martin. And we are very much aware of what is happening. So, no, you're not that good."

Haydeez chuckled. "But," she paused. "You need my help. Knowing what's happening and knowing how to stop it are completely different. So," she paused again. "Are you ready to ask for my help?"

"Enough," Agent Red said. "If you allow us to come in, we can discuss this further. Standing out on the side of the road is not exactly 'private'."

Haydeez sighed. "You've got a point." She walked to a panel and covered the keys. The gate creaked open. "Don't take this as a welcome," she said as she motioned them inside.

The agents passed through the gates. Steam passed from his lips as Agent Red spoke. "Yes, we know something is going on. Yes, we are more than capable of," he paused and removed his jacket. "Taking care of ourselves." Two black metallic wings spread out and flexed. His clothing was tight across his chest. He rolled his neck. "We just need to know where to go."

"So, you're just a loaded gun until someone points you and pulls the trigger," Linx said.

Agent Red shot Linx a look. His eyes were wide, but not in fear. It looked as if his mind had run through different scenarios of how to kill Linx. His wings moved with a life of their own. The metallic feathers slid across each other with the soft whisper of polished steel on steel. They pulsed and breathed as he moved, the way a bird's wings would, and conformed to his back.

"Let's play nice, boys," Haydeez said. She turned toward Agent Red and asked, "Born with those or given that lovely gift?"

Agent Red turned to Haydeez. "Do you know anyone born with metal sprouting from their shoulder blades?" he asked.

With a smirk, she retorted, "I don't know. Have I just met someone who was?" Before he could respond, she turned to Agent Blue. "Do you have shiny wings too or do you have other hidden talents?"

Agent Blue tapped her head and said, "Hidden talents. But we're not really here for that. Obviously, you're a step ahead. Somehow we seem to be missing something. So," she said and crossed her arms. "What are we missing?"

"If I knew what you had, I could tell you where your mistakes are but I'm not going to sit here and go back and forth about who has what information and whether or not you actually need something, or if you should even have it. We're a little beyond that at this point. We don't have the time and I certainly don't have the patience," Haydeez said as Linx snorted back a laugh. Haydeez ignored him and continued. "At this point, I already know that I know more than you because you're the ones watching me. So," she said and crossed her arms. "This is how it's going to be. You will stay out of my way. I have a job to do and whether you're there or not, I'm going to do it. The problem I have is with you being in my way. You see, I fight. I know how Linx fights, but you... I don't know you and I can't risk you getting in the middle of the fight and end up getting one of us killed because of your stupidity." She eyed both of the agents. "I need to beat her to save humanity. I don't know how yet but I know I will do it."

Agent Blue returned Haydeez's stare. "Need to beat who?" she asked.

"Really? Wow, you're less informed than I imagined," Linx said. "Pandora. You know, destroyer of man and all that. That's who we're after. That's who we need to stop."

Agent Red stepped in. "And why do you believe we will get in the way?" he asked impatiently.

Haydeez shook her head and chuckled. "Because you didn't even know who we're fighting. You don't even have all the information. Do you know what she's planning? I do. Do you know what she's done? I do. Have you watched a woman's life slip from her body while she begged for you to just make it all end, to let death take her because that was better than the agony she was in, and it was all because of something Pandora did?" She paused as Linx silently put his hand on her shoulder. "I have," she added through gritted teeth. "I've seen what she's capable of and you need to realize something. All she cares about is destroying man. How everyone dies doesn't matter. She's letting out some of the most hateful, malicious creatures you can dream up and it's not just a quick painless death. It's slow torture. It's children being ripped apart and eaten. It's millions of miscarriages all at once so blood flows freely. Check the news if you haven't already seen it. The entire city of Boston was decimated. I couldn't even save a single person. Do you get it now? I can't afford to have you in my way. I need to stop her before she makes good on her promise."

The agents looked at each other for a moment. Agent Blue asked, "Do you know how to stop her?"

Haydeez rubbed her face and groaned. "Again, no I don't, not yet, but I'm confident that we will figure it out." She looked back and forth between the agents again. "What? I highly doubt you know how to take care of her."

"No, we don't but it seems reckless to go against her without a plan in place," Agent Red responded. "Normally I wouldn't criticize but if this is actually who you say, we need to be more organized in any approach."

"*If? We?*" Haydeez scoffed. "I didn't invite you along for the ride, did I?" she yelled. "What I said is that I don't want you in my way. And as far as being who I said, yea, doubt me if you want to. I don't care. I'll go save the world and you can wonder what happened in your lives that led you to this point. So, now that we've shared our information, why don't you leave?" She motioned to the front gate.

Agent Blue shook her head. "Not a chance. We were assigned to you specifically. So, we don't leave until our orders change. Travel where you want, but just know that we will follow."

Linx watched the exchange between the two women. He took a step back in case Haydeez decided to take a swing. "You want to hang around. What exactly do you plan on doing? I mean, you're not prepared with information. Have you ever fought someone created just to destroy the human race? Do you have experience with Pandora's box? I don't get why we should trust you as our back-up just at face value."

Agent Red clenched his fists and jerked forward. Agent Blue blocked him with her arm and said, "We'll be in touch, Ms. Blackhawk." She turned to Linx. "Mr. Van Martin," she added with a smirk and a slight nod. With her hand on Agent Red's arm, she guided him towards the gate. Without a word, they walked off the property to their vehicle and drove away.

Steam rose from her skin as Haydeez watched them leave. The cold air danced over her flesh but her anger sent it away in tiny, white wisps.

"We're never getting rid of them are we?" Linx asked.

"Looks that way," Haydeez responded. She closed the front gate and they headed back inside.

"Probably a good thing that you didn't mention you've actually spoken to Pandora," Linx joked.

Epilogue

Haydeez looked around the empty parking garage. She closed her eyes and listened. "Don't say anything for a minute," she whispered. Her head cocked to the side and she slowly turned in a circle. "Where are you?" she whispered again. A smile spread across her lips. "I hear you." She opened her eyes and clicked the device in her hand.

"All clear, love," Linx said. "Cameras are black and the clock's ticking."

"Perfect," she said and took off at a run. She jumped onto the wall of the spiral drive and dropped down to the next level. With her body crouched low to the ground, she smelled the air. Damp cement and the leftover exhaust of hundreds of cars almost covered the scent of reptile. An overhead light flickered at the other end of the garage as she scanned the level. "Can't hide from me, snake lady. I know you're here," she mumbled.

There was movement at the edge of her vision and she turned quickly.

Euryale slithered over the side of the wall and hissed. "You do not know when to quit do you? What must I do to convince you that you cannot beat me?" She flashed her fangs and hissed again. "I had planned to spare you but I suppose tasting your muddied blood is preferable to being followed by you for the rest of my days."

"Seventeen minutes left, love," Linx said.

"Plenty of time," she answered. A dull grey blade rolled slowly between her fingertips as she smiled. "I brought an old friend to the party this time. No guns, just pure iron. Found out this handy little trinket can do some serious damage to your kind. Hunt's over, Euryale."

Euryale leaned back on her tail, muscles bunched. "You cannot hurt me, mutt," she hissed. "My hunt is not over. It has just become interesting.

I enjoy it when my prey puts up a fight." She sprang forward, claws out, mouth open, and grabbed for Haydeez.

Haydeez jumped towards Euryale at the same time and swiped up with the iron dagger. She slashed open the gorgon's flesh on the inside of her bicep. "Felt good, didn't it?" she asked with a chuckle.

Euryale glared at Haydeez. "How did you do that? Your flimsy mortal weapon should not be able to hurt me!" she yelled. As she clutched her arm, she hissed and leaned back on her tail again. "That will be your only strike, mutt." She sprang forward again and swung her good arm across her body to strike.

Haydeez rolled to the side and popped up into a crouch. Before Euryale had the chance to turn, Haydeez pounced on her from the side.

"Twelve minutes left," Linx said.

"Working on it," Haydeez grumbled. She clung to Euryale's side as the gorgon swung her arms around. Haydeez stabbed the dagger into Euryale's hip.

The gorgon screamed in pain. She swung her tail and smacked Haydeez off. She slammed her tail down right in the middle of the hunter's chest and knocked the wind out. With a groan and a hiss, she looked at Haydeez. "Vermin!" she howled. "How dare you strike one who is better than you!" She slammed her tail down again.

Haydeez gasped for air. She grabbed at her throat as her weak voice croaked out of her throat. "Linx," she said, her words barely above a whisper.

Euryale grabbed at her side and turned toward the wall. She slithered forward with all the strength she had left and lifted her battered body over the cement barrier. Her tail dropped over the side by the time Haydeez got to her feet and finally managed to speak.

"Damn it!" Haydeez yelled. She cleared her throat a few times. "How much time is left?" she asked, aggravation apparent in her voice.

"Six minutes left, love. Cutting it a little close. You've got to get out of there soon," Linx said.

Haydeez growled. "I've got this." She ran to the spot Euryale went over and swung her legs over. Her toes touched the floor beneath and her body dropped. She crouched with her face almost on the concrete. Drops of blood sprinkled the ground around her. "Shh," she breathed. Her body stretched out across the floor. She slid like a lioness across the grass as she followed the blood. Her heartbeat slowed. She exhaled as she stretched out her body again. Her moves were precise and intentional. As she inhaled, the scent of reptile was stronger.

Euryale sat curled in a dark corner. She held her side with one hand and licked the open wound on her arm.

Haydeez released a slow and steady breath as she pulled her body forward once more. A wicked smile spread across her lips.

"Two minutes left," Linx whispered. "Get it done and get out now."

"Shh," Haydeez breathed again. Her muscles tightened and she adjusted her body. In one swift movement, she pounced on Euryale.

The gorgon yelled.

Haydeez slashed with the dagger and sliced open Euryale's other arm. The gorgon fell to the ground and shrieked. Haydeez landed on top of her. She put the iron dagger against Euryale's throat and whispered, "You didn't really think I'd just let you go, did you?" The dagger squished into the gorgon's neck. Haydeez jumped up and said, "Like I said before, hunt's over." She turned and ran to the wall. She leaned over the side and said, "Three floors. I can make it."

"Three floors? Wait, what?" Linx yelled.

Before he could stop her, Haydeez had thrown herself over the side and dropped to the wall beneath and continued to hop down till she reached the ground. With a grunt she said, "Yup, just three floors."

The stop watch flashed zero. "Times up," Linx said. "Did you really just jump down three floors of a parking garage? Are you completely insane?"

Haydeez laughed. "Must be because I just killed something else and gave her more power." She started to walk towards where she parked. "You know I thought it would be cooler here. It's further south and all. Do you think this will all go back to normal once we stop her? I mean, I love the snow but this is getting ridiculous." She took a deep breath and let it out slowly.

"Probably," Linx answered. "I would think so since she's the reason for everything. It started with that weird tornado explosion thing at the museum. I hope this isn't permanent. Bebo is not happy with it and he's taking it out on me. Do you know how hard he can head-butt? I bet you don't because he doesn't do it to you."

"You're going to have to get along with him. I can't intervene all the time," Haydeez said with a chuckle. Then, with a groan she added, "It's going to be a long night. I'm not looking forward to this drive."

About the Author

Rebecca Flynn has always had a love for mythologies and the creatures of legends. Reading has always been an integral part of her life. There are books in every room of her home. When she's not writing, she's spending time with her four children and five dogs in the mountains of Eastern Tennessee.

Note from the Author

Word-of-mouth is crucial for any author to succeed. If you enjoyed *Iron Will*, please leave a review online—anywhere you are able. Even if it's just a sentence or two. It would make all the difference and would be very much appreciated.

Thanks!
Rebecca Flynn

Thank you so much for reading one of Rebecca Flynn's novels.
If you enjoyed the experience, please check out Book 1 of
The Pandora Chronicles for your next great read!

The Wild Hunted by Rebecca Flynn

"A mixture of Celtic mythology, action, adventure,
and suspense, this page-turner will keep you
on the edge of your seat from cover to cover!"
—Erin Danzer, author of the *Spiral Defenders Series*